The Ghost
AND
Mrs. McClure

The Ghost
AND
Mrs. McClure

Alice Kimberly

WHEELER
CHIVERS

This Large Print edition is published by Wheeler Publishing, Waterville, Maine USA and by BBC Audiobooks, Ltd, Bath, England.

Published in 2004 in the U.S. by arrangement with The Berkley Publishing Group, a member of Penguin Group (USA) Inc.

Published in 2004 in the U.K. by arrangement with The Berkley Publishing Group, a division of Penguin Group (USA) Inc.

U.S. Softcover   1-58724-666-X   (Cozy Mystery)
U.K. Hardcover 1-4056-3007-8   (Chivers Large Print)
U.K. Softcover   1-4056-3008-6   (Camden Large Print)

The text of this Large Print edition is unabridged.
Other aspects of the book may vary from the original edition.

Set in 16 pt. Plantin by Minnie B. Raven.

Printed in the United States on permanent paper.

British Library Cataloguing-in-Publication Data available

Library of Congress Cataloging-in-Publication Data

Kimberly, Alice.
    The ghost and Mrs. McClure / Alice Kimberly.
        p. cm.
    ISBN 1-58724-666-X (lg. print : sc : alk. paper)
    1. Women booksellers — Fiction.   2. Novelists —
Crimes against — Fiction.   3. Rhode Island — Fiction.
4. Widows — Fiction.   5. Large type books.   I. Title.
PS3611.I458G47 2004
    813′.6—dc22   2004045520

†

The Ghost

AND

Mrs. McClure

Acknowledgments

The author wishes to thank
Senior Editor Kimberly Lionetti
and literary agent John Talbot
for their valued support in giving this distinct
physical incarnation to
what began as the ghost of an idea.

And

very special thanks to
Major John J. Leyden, Jr.
Field Operations Officer,
Rhode Island State Police
for his helpful answers
to procedural questions.

Author's Note

Although real places and institutions are mentioned in this book, they are used in the service of fiction. No character in this book is based on any person, living or dead, and the world presented is completely fictitious.

Contents

"You mean there is a hell?" asked Lucy.
"Some people might call it so," said
    the captain.
"There's a dimension that some spirits
    have to wait in till they realize and
    admit the truth about themselves."
                — R. A. Dick,
                    The Ghost and Mrs. Muir

Prologue

My life is my own, and the opinions of others don't interest me . . .
— Carroll John Daly, "Three Gun Terry," *Black Mask*, May 1923 (cited as the first published appearance of a hard-boiled detective)

Quindicott, Rhode Island
1949

Cranberry. What kind of a cornball name was that for a street?

Jack Shepard hauled his powerful frame out of the black Packard and slammed the heavy door, sending a violent shudder through the mass of metal.

Five hours. He'd just spent five dusty hours behind the wheel of this boiler, hunched up like some luckless clipster trying to crack a bag man's safe.

With easy fingers, Jack button-closed his double-breasted jacket. The suit was gunmetal gray, rising in a V from his narrow waist to his acre of shoulders. Closing his eyes, he imagined a pretty set of hands working over the kinks and knots. Tonight,

13

thought Jack. After the drive back to Manhattan's crowded dirty noise, he'd find a willing pair in some suds club, like he always did.

Casing the scene, Jack scanned the two- and three-story buildings that lined this lane — a kiddie version of the towering steel and glass where he usually ranged. "Town," he muttered. That's what two farmers had called it about ten miles back, out by the cow pasture and old mill, where he'd asked for directions. The "Welcome to Quindicott" sign came next. Farmland after, more of the monotonous rolling green he'd driven through on the way up. Then came the gradual density of houses. Trees and lawns and hedges trimmed by do-right guys. Barking dogs and chubby-cheeked kids. You had your "quaint" town square, your manicured lawn, and your white bandshell with red trim. The whole thing looked so doggone cheery, Jack expected to see a Norman Rockwell signature in the sidewalk.

The "townsfolk" in this homespun little picture looked cheery enough, too, soaking up the last hours of the orange sun's late-summer juice. Young men in flannel. Old men with clay pipes. Farmers' wives in gingham, and shop girls with bare legs.

These people were off the cob, all right, Jack thought, starting a casual stroll. Corny as they came. Some rocked on porches, some gabbed on benches, some ambled along the cobblestone lane — and all eyes were on him —

"*Who are ya, fella?*"

Curious eyes —

"*Waddaya want?*"

Small-town eyes —

"*Ya don't belong.*"

Jack lit a butt from his deck of Luckies, then used a single finger to push back his fedora. *You people want a look at my mug? Go on then, look.*

Jack's face wasn't pretty, but no dame ever complained. His forehead was broad with thick sandy brows; his cheeks were sunken, and his nose like a boxer's — slightly crooked with a broken-a-few-times bump. His jaw was iron, his chin flat and square — with a one-inch scar in the shape of a dagger slashing across it — and his eyes were sharper than a skiv. Freddie once told him they were the color of granite and just about as hard.

Maybe he was hard, thought Jack. But baby, this was one hick town. No painted dolls or groghounds here. No nickel rats, cheap grifters, or diamond-dripping dames looking to have their husbands set up. Just clean air, families with kids, potluck socials, and farm-fresh moo juice.

A town for settling down. That's what this place was, thought Jack. A few of those bare-legged, unpainted country dolls passed him, gave him the shy version of the "what's-*your-name-big-fella?*" once-over. *Nice,* thought Jack, eyeballing them right back. Shapely gams. Milky skin. Curves the way he liked them — bountiful. Jack took a long, slow drag from his Lucky and turned away. A man like him had to be careful in a place like this. Say the right thing to the wrong broad and he'd make her about a thousand times more miserable than he was.

With a slight limp, Jack continued his slow stroll — casual, easy, hands in pockets, the ache in his shin an unwanted souvenir from that underpaid job he'd done for Uncle Sam over in Germany. Jack ignored it. Continued to case the scene.

Ahead of him, a row of shops beckoned. Bakery, grocery, dress joint, beauty parlor. There it was: one twenty-two. A little more class than the other places. Probably did business with that fancy Newport set not far away. Wide plate-glass window. Words etched in: We Buy and Sell Books.

Yeah. But did they have the book he was looking for? The one *they* were looking for? The one they killed Freddie for?

The sun was sinking like a popped balloon now. The day was done, the lights nearly out, and just around the corner, a shadow stained the sidewalk, a city-suited figure, waiting.

Jack cursed low. Thought he'd shaken that tail.

He turned the brass handle, pushed. The shop's bell tinkled like a bad girl's giggle. A chill up his spine like a foot on his grave.

The shadow moved closer.

Jack's hand rose, dipped into his suitcoat, caressed his rod's handle, smooth from wear. He got a bad feeling, but Jack had gotten them before. And when he started a thing, he never turned back.

Besides, this job was for Freddie, and Jack promised his dead friend he'd ride this train out. All the way to the end of the line.

I stake my everlasting life on it.

When the shadow receded, Jack refocused his attention on the job at hand. Investigation and interrogation were things he'd polished as a private eye, but he'd learned as a cop — back before he'd joined up. In the service, he'd learned a lot more: About men and the things they'd do and say under pressure. About the enemy: how and why they'd lie, and, more importantly, what methods would pry the truth out of them.

The moment of truth came today.

For Jack it came sharp and hard and quick, landing at the back of his skull. But the blow didn't kill him. The gunshots did. To the head, to the face, to the heart. Enough to make sure Jack Shepard's everlasting promise to his friend began today . . . along with his everlasting life.

Chapter 1

The Big Ending

Murder doesn't round out anybody's life, except the murdered and sometimes the murderer's.
— Nick Charles to Nora Charles in *The Thin Man* by Dashiell Hammett, 1933

Quindicott, Rhode Island
Today

"We killed him!"

I was beside myself. In a frantic state of hand-wringing and head-shaking, I paced the length of the bookshop's aisle from Christie to Grafton and back again.

"Calm down, dear," said my aunt, her slight frame tipping the Shaker rocker back and forth with about as much anxiety as a retiree on a Palm Beach sundeck.

"*How* can I calm down?" I asked. "We killed a best-selling author on the first night of his book tour!"

"Well, the milk's gone and spilled now. No use crying over it. If you need help calming down, why don't you have a belt?"

I was not surprised by this rather unladylike suggestion from my aunt. Sadie may have been seventy-two, and barely four feet eleven, but for an aging bantamweight she had a big mouth and a good right hook. The Quindicott Business Owners' Association never forgot the day she'd spotted a shoplifter at ten yards (putting a Hammett first edition down his pants). She'd taken him out with one sharp Patricia Cornwell to the head.

For decades, Sadie had run the bookstore as modestly as her late father had. Never once had she considered holding an author appearance like this one. It was stupid, presumptuous *me*, Mrs. Penelope Thornton "Know It All" McClure, who'd tried to bring twenty-first-century bookselling to Quindicott.

Why? Why in the world did I think I could pull it off?

Sure, right after college I had taken a job in the hard-nosed offices of New York City book publishing. But I hadn't exactly been wildly successful at it (my nose being as squashy as a Stay Puft marshmallow). The one thing I thought I *had* gotten from the experience was the knowledge of how to create a hospitable, crowd-drawing store on the book tour circuit.

Of course, that was before Timothy Brennan — the very first best-selling author we were lucky enough to host — began

19

choking in the middle of his televised lecture, then commenced flailing around like a big Irish goldfish ejected from its bowl, and finally dropped dead as a doorknob in the middle of the bookstore's brand-new community events space.

"Someone get my niece a drink!" Aunt Sadie called from her rocker.

Linda Cooper-Logan heeded Sadie's call. In her thirties, her short platinum hair still in the spiky, punkish style she'd first worn in the eighties, Linda appeared in a long, flowery skirt and worn denim jacket. Her jade and silver bracelets jangled as she held out a bottle of carrot juice. I reached for it, but Sadie interceded.

"Not *that* kind of drink," said my aunt. "A *real* drink."

"Oh!" said Linda. She put two fingers in her mouth. A sharp whistle caught the attention of Linda's husband, Milner Logan. He was at the other end of the store, watching Officers Eddie Franzetti and Welsh Tibbet — one-quarter of the entire patrol division of Quindicott's lilliputian police department — take down the names of guests who hadn't already fled, and few had. After all, what better spectacle could be found tonight in the entire state of Rhode Island? Anyone present knew their "I watched Timothy Brennan drop dead" story would render them good as gold at every church social and backyard barbecue for the next ten years.

"Are you puckering up and blowing for me, Linda?" asked Milner sweetly. Quarter-blood Narragansett Native American, Milner frequented our store for crime novels, noir thrillers, and the occasional frontlist Tony Hillerman. Like his wife, he'd held on to some fashion trends of his own youth — a decade before Linda's. He wore a small gold hoop in his left ear and his long hair in a ponytail, the strands looking more wiry salt-and-pepper these days than midnight black.

Together Linda and Milner ran the Cooper Family Bakery here in Quindicott. Linda handled the comfort food; Milner, the fancy French stuff. (He and Linda had met when Milner was teaching a cooking school class in Boston on the art of French pastry. Linda fell for him over a perfectly mixed ball of *pâte sablée*.)

Having their baked goods as part of to-night's hospitality refreshments had been a coup for the bookstore. Milner had added French touches to so many of the old Cooper family recipes, the result was a table of goodies to die for — and, unfortunately, tonight someone actually had.

"We need a drink for Penelope!" Linda called to her husband.

"Oh?" Milner strolled closer in his fedora and double-breasted gray suit — like many of those who'd attended tonight's event, Milner

21

had come dressed as Jack Shield, the hard-boiled detective star of Timothy Brennan's internationally best-selling series.

And I'd actually encouraged it.

From Providence and Boston to high-toned Newport and Greenwich, the newspaper ads I'd placed invited Brennan's fans to come dressed as the famous hard-boiled detective. Every fan knew how Jack Shield dressed, of course, because Shield had been based on a real private investigator of the late 1940s named Jack Shepard. And Shepard's chilling, anvil-chinned grimace appeared (in black-and-white) on the back flap of every Brennan dust jacket, right under the author's own photo (in living color).

"You mean the hard stuff? Joy juice? Hooch?" asked Milner, nudging up the front brim of his fedora one-finger style, like Shield.

"Oh, for heaven's sake!" cried Sadie. "Just get the bottle from under the register already!"

Milner brought over the bottle of whiskey and a few paper cups. Sadie poured shots all around. "After the shock of tonight's events, I'd say we could all use a belt."

I didn't want to partake, but Sadie pressed the cup into my wringing hands. "Now, Penelope, honey, listen to your elder. *Drink.*"

I did. The liquid burned, but I trusted my aunt knew what was best at the moment —

at least she seemed much calmer than I.

"Feel better?" asked Sadie.

"Don't worry, Pen," said Milner. "I over-heard Eddie say there's going to be an autopsy, because it's a suspicious death. It's just like a crime novel. Kinda cool, actually."

"What killed him?" I said, noting that the room was both too bright and too dark. Was that possible?

Milner shrugged.

I took another swig from the cup. "What's going to happen, do you think?" I asked. "Because of Timothy Brennan's death, I mean. Do you think we should close the store? Forever?"

He shrugged again.

I took another swig.

Hard liquor was new to me. A glass of white wine or light beer once a month or so was my usual consumption rate. Whiskey, it would seem, sure hit faster than Chardonnay.

Linda and Milner were speaking, saying something like all this was in no way the store's fault, and I should just go on as if nothing had happened. But their voices seemed as fuzzy as their faces. And then the room began a slow spin.

How could this have happened? I wondered. How?

I'd worked so hard to prepare. Just two hours ago, everything had been in perfect order . . . just two hours ago . . .

Chapter 2

The Author Arrives

[N]ice men often write bad verse and good poets can be monsters. . . . It seemed easier all around not to be able to put a face to a name, and judge solely on the printed page.
— A. Alvarez, *The Savage God: A Study in Suicide*

Two Hours Ago . . .

"How are things going?" I asked my aunt as she rang up — thank the ISBN gods! — four *Shield of Justice* purchases for one of the early guests now browsing the stacks. Timothy Brennan was scheduled to appear in exactly fifty-three minutes, and I was trying not to worry.

I had dressed with care in a crisply ironed black skirt, baby blue short-sleeved sweater set, nude stockings, and slingback heels. Sadie had made an effort, too. She'd actually brought out one of her few dresses — the belted, pine green number that matched her eyes and complemented her short gray hair, colored auburn and accented at Colleen's Beauty Shop with "Shirley MacLaine" strawberry blond highlights.

"Hard to tell how things are going," said my aunt. "Not many arrivals yet."

"This event will bring us heaps of new business. You'll see," I told her.

"Well, if it doesn't, look on the bright side. We can stack those three hundred hardcovers in the back room straight up to the part of the ceiling where it's starting to droop and call it a literary pillar."

"That's not funny."

"Okay. We'll burn them for kindling, then. We haven't used that potbellied stove on the back porch since my father was breathing."

"*Still* not funny," I said. "And you know very well we'd have to return them unsold or else pay the publisher fifty-four percent of each copy's retail cover price."

"So we'll burn the invoices and overdue notices then," Sadie said. "Either way, dear, if this shindig doesn't bring in new business, we're going to need something to keep us warm this winter."

I inspected the floor display we'd unpacked and assembled hours earlier. The dump was typical corrugate from the publisher, with a big image of the book's cover and the handsome author photo that appeared on every one of Brennan's dust jackets. Space for twelve hardcovers also was provided — four face-outs, three deep.

One of the books seemed a tad out of line. I adjusted the angle, then fiddled with the life-size cut-out display of the handsome author. Timothy Brennan had sandy blond hair and a charming grin. His standee image looked about forty and very fit.

True, he had to be older than the photo, but some men aged very well, never losing their virility (I wouldn't turn down a date with Sean Connery or Clint Eastwood, for instance), and I'm embarrassed to admit I'd developed a bit of a crush on Mr. Brennan.

"Have you actually seen Mr. Brennan yet?" I asked, resisting the urge to chew my thumbnail.

"No, dear," said Sadie. "But I noticed —" Sadie paused to let out a little sneeze.

"Bless you," I said.

"Thank you," she said. "I was about to say — I noticed an older man who looked a little like Brennan. Maybe he was an older relative. He came in with three well-dressed people —" This second sneeze was so sudden her glasses fell from the end of her nose to dangle from the string of red beads around her neck.

"Bless you," I said again.

A vile stench tickled my own nose. A *cigar,* I realized with a shudder. Obviously someone was ignoring the *No Smoking* signs posted all over the store.

I'd find the offender and set him straight, but I wanted to check on Spencer first. He was wandering around in his little gray Brooks Brothers pinstripes.

"You look very handsome," I told him, my maternal pride gushing forth.

"Yes, Mother, you said that already."

Spencer remained less than thrilled with our move up to Rhode Island. But I couldn't blame him, really. His seven years on earth had been spent living in a luxurious Manhattan apartment. Our move forced him to live in six small, run-down rooms above an old bookstore with the looming prospect of *public* school — an institution his wealthy in-laws had convinced him mainly housed potential convicts.

Tonight, we'd actually argued about his coming downstairs. He insisted on watching TV. I insisted he get dressed and show some support of what was now our family business.

Actually, my bookstore-owning days had started about three months ago. Standing in the marble lobby of my doorman building, I'd been reading Aunt Sadie's periodic letter about the local goings-on in Quindicott when my gaze locked on her casual postscript: *By the way, the store is about to go belly up and I'll be closing the doors in a few weeks.*

I'd phoned her that day, the modest check from the life insurance policy of my late husband, Calvin, in my hand, and proposed we go into business together.

Two weeks later, after Spencer finished second grade at the expensive private school Calvin and his family had insisted he attend (with a faculty so pompous and intimidating I practically needed one of Calvin's Valiums to get through Parents' Night), I moved us out of the posh McClure-owned penitentiary on Manhattan's Upper East Side and into my aunt's humble walk-up. Now, at least, I could raise my son in peace — that is, without the thinly veiled financial threats of my in-laws.

My own income, working at a publishing house, had been modest, and Calvin had never worked — his income having been supplied by his wealthy mother. So the life insurance money was practically all I had now.

Apart from my young son's trust fund, which I was legally forbidden to touch, no inheritance or any "financial aid" would come my way unless I agreed to remain under the thumb of the McClures and their opinions, which actually included the idea of an English boarding school for my little boy.

(Excuse me? Not now. Not ever.)

So I'd shocked them all by packing up and moving beyond their hypercritical gazes. Now I was a full-fledged co-owner of my own failing business. And I was determined to remake it from top to bottom.

To Sadie's credit, from the day I'd arrived,

she stood back and let me. Buy the Book hadn't even been the original name of the place. Personally, I'd liked the old Thornton's sign, which stated in that unadorned, pragmatic way of the 1940s: We Buy and Sell Books. But the past was *dead,* and our future depended on recognizing this.

"If we're going to attract those book-buying urban dwellers with wads of disposable income," I'd explained to my aunt, "we've got to have a name that's postmodern."

"What do you mean? Something cutesy? Like Bookends?"

"No. Something more deliberately ironic and self-aware. Remember, the elite, *über*educated generation of today disdains literal plain speaking. We must find a name that has a double meaning."

"Double meaning?"

"Something slick and smart aleck-esque, you know? Something a precocious kid might think was funny."

Aunt Sadie nodded. "In that case, let's ask Spencer."

So I called up to my bright little boy.

"Yes? What do you want?" Spencer yelled from the upstairs window with the perfect diction of a privately schooled New York child.

"Come down and help us rename the store," said Sadie.

"But Sergeant Friday's getting ready to book the bad guy!"

"Well, dear, after the man is cuffed, come on down!"

From the day we'd moved in with Sadie, Spence wanted to do little more than watch old cop shows on Sadie's new digital cable and stroke the marmalade-striped kitten she'd given him.

I loved the kitten, but I was worried about his watching so much television. On the other hand, Spence was still adjusting to a lot, so I saw no harm in indulging him a little — although this cop show obsession was truly peculiar. I couldn't recall Spence ever having such an interest.

Then again, how would I have known? Calvin had refused to allow a television in any room of our apartment — he claimed it stressed his nerves, but then almost everything did, including Spencer himself.

You know the pathetic truth? The truth I'd never admit to anyone? Calvin Spencer McClure III had been a lousy father. But he'd been the only father Spence had known, and Spence missed him.

So when Spence came downstairs, the three of us brainstormed.

" 'Booked' . . . 'You're Booked' . . . 'Central Booking' . . .'" I threw out, because our store specialized in mysteries.

"Why not just 'By the Book'?" suggested Spencer, who'd just heard the phrase on *Dragnet*.

30

"That's it! That's perfect!" I said. "Only we'll spell it 'B-u-y.' "

" 'Buy the Book.' " Sadie shrugged. "Okay, whatever you think will help business, dear. But don't help it too much. This town's got parking problems, you know."

(What Sadie actually said was *"pahkin' problems."* The "Roe Dyelin" accent is sometimes light, sometimes heavy, but pretty much incomprehensible when written out on paper. Car, pocket, pasta, meatballs, letter, chowder, and Europe would sound more like cah, parkit, pahster, meatbowls, letta, chowda, and Yerp. You'll just have to trust me going with the conventional spellings on this one.)

So anyway, the hip new name on a hip new sign went up on the shop and the rest of the life insurance money went into a new beveled glass door, front window, and awning. Out went the ancient fluorescent ceiling fixtures and old metal shelves. In their place I put track lighting, an eclectic array of antique floor and table lamps, and oak bookcases.

I restored the chestnut-stained wood plank floor, and throughout the stacks, I scattered overstuffed armchairs and Shaker-style rockers to give customers the feeling of browsing through a New Englander's private library.

Finally, I overhauled the inventory, keeping the store's original rare book business but adding plenty of mysteries along with some New England travel guides and Yankee cookbooks.

I had hoped the BMWs, Jaguars, and Mercedes rocketing through Quindicott for gas fill-ups on their way to the resort towns of Cape Cod or Newport would pause to check out the "quaint"-looking mystery-themed bookshop. But they hadn't.

Sadly, the years of economic booms and busts had taken their toll on "Old Q," and many of the shops on Cranberry had become run down, not just our bookstore.

Empty storefronts didn't help, either, and we had one right next door. People had taken to calling it "cursed," not only for hosting the most "going out of business" sales in Quindicott, but also for being "haunted." (Ridiculous, of course.)

Not yet ready to lie down and die, I decided what we needed were some well-publicized book-related events and the space to stage them. So I mortgaged Buy the Book to purchase the so-called cursed storefront adjoining ours, expanding the bookstore to its original size for the first time in fifty years.

Now Buy the Book occupied the entire freestanding stone building at 122. And, lord, was I proud!

Okay, so it was a huge financial risk. "Like betting on the horsies," to quote Sadie exactly. But we hit it big right out of the gate because, for some reason, the legendary Timothy Brennan had chosen our little Quindicott shop to kick off his big national book tour, promoting *Shield of Justice*, the latest novel in his famous series.

Tonight was the make-or-break moment for Buy the Book, and I was determined to see that it came off without a hitch.

I bent down to adjust Spencer's blue-and-silver striped tie, which seemed just slightly off center. As I wiggled the knot, Spencer stared at the ceiling and let his hands fall to his sides like a tiny Wall Street rag doll. It reminded me of a remark he'd made last Christmas to one of his little friends in the lobby of our building while Calvin, Spencer, and I waited for a cab to Lincoln Center: "Once my mother starts with the fixing, resistance is futile."

"Now, Spencer, remember what we talked about," I said as gently as possible. I was feeling bad enough for making him put on the suit and come downstairs.

"I'll behave, Mother. I told you already."

"No tricks."

"I *told* you ten times. I did not do *anything* to the chairs."

"I know, honey. I just can't explain it otherwise."

"Well, I wish you wouldn't go blaming me

just because you don't have a perp to fit your profile."

My eyebrow rose. Maybe Spence *was* watching too many of those TV cop shows. Well, I thought, at least it's a sign he might *one day* show some interest in our store.

With a sigh, I brushed his copper bangs, made a note that they were getting long again, and nodded. When I'd first come downstairs, after showering and changing, I had found all the chairs in the community events space — the chairs I'd *painstakingly* arranged into rows rectilinear enough for a military parade ground — turned upside down.

I'd raced back upstairs to find Spencer watching an old *Mike Hammer* episode. My son had claimed innocence. So I went to find Sadie.

Once she'd put on her shoes and found her belt, she came downstairs with me to see "the deed for herself," as she'd put it. Spencer had already gone downstairs to look, and we'd found him just standing there in the community events space, staring.

"Mom," he'd said, "there's nothing wrong with the chairs."

In no more than five minutes, all the chairs had been righted again.

Now, a seven-year-old boy may have been able to turn over one hundred chairs upside down in forty-five minutes, I'd thought, but not in five.

"Do you think you imagined it?" Sadie had asked me.

"No. I did not," I'd told her. "I know what I saw. And five minutes ago, those chairs were upside down."

Sadie gave me a sidelong glance.

"I was *not* hallucinating."

"Must be the ghost," she'd said with a shrug.

"The ghost?" I'd said.

"Sure. Quite a few stories like yours over the years with this part of the building. Even the construction boys had some strange things happen, you have to admit."

Okay, so during the renovations some of the workmen complained about vanishing tools and unexplained power surges. But I'd chalked all of it up to ancient wiring and maybe Spencer playing a practical joke with the hardware.

"Goes to show how gullible some of us can be," I'd muttered, annoyed by the accelerated pounding of my stupid heart.

"Some say ghosts can affect your senses," Sadie had pointed out. "Make you see things that aren't there . . . see things the way they want you to see them."

"Humbug" had been my muttered reply. "What are we? Cavewomen? We see lightning and right away think some sky god is angry at us?"

Sadie had just shrugged again. Then we'd

searched the entire building for some intruder. But there'd been none. And the doors and windows had all been secure.

"No more ghost talk," I'd told her when she gave me an annoyingly knowing look. "There is no ghost here. Some hand turned those chairs. Some *human* hand."

But whose? I still wondered.

Could Spencer really have been so disturbed and angry that he'd managed to pull off a nearly impossible prank for a boy of his size and age — turning them first upside down, then, in mere minutes, right side up again?

"That's right!" a loud voice suddenly boomed from the new events space. "Let's get this crap out of the way."

I told Spence to help Aunt Sadie at the register. Then I rushed over to the adjoining storefront in time to see a padded folding chair clatter to the wood plank floor.

"Good lord," I muttered, "not my chairs again!"

My gaze lifted to the center of the events room. There, shouting commands to a trio of well-dressed people, stood a man in his seventies: Timothy Brennan.

I hadn't recognized him at first because he looked at least twenty-five years older than the photos on his book jacket, floor display, *and* life-size standee. His hair was gray and thin; his bushy brows crowned bloodshot

36

eyes; and his ruddy, jowl-framed face reflected the hundred additional pounds he was now carrying.

Two young men in baggy jeans and flapping flannel suddenly barreled into the room, carrying a video camera, tripod, and heavy silver cases. Mr. Brennan waved his pudgy finger under their noses.

"The camera goes on my right," Brennan garbled to them around a foul-smelling cigar. "I want those lucky C-SPAN book TV viewers to see my best side." Then he glanced at the well-dressed couple moving my meticulously arranged refreshment table. "Come on, Ken, move that thing already! We haven't got all night!"

The staccato thumping of a dozen plastic water bottles came next. I had personally set them on the goodies table near the room's entrance to make our guests feel welcome. Juices, sodas, and plastic bottles of Sutter Spring water now tumbled to the floor as the man named Ken, and a well-dressed woman about his age, jostled the table toward the back of the room.

Ken was fiftyish with salt-and-pepper hair and silver temples, model-perfect features, and a well-tailored camel-haired jacket that flattered his strong physique. The middle-aged woman, holding the other end, was a slender redhead whose impeccably tailored burgundy suit and matching scarf helped take the bite out of her otherwise very plain face.

Another woman, much younger, wearing a chic black pantsuit with a very pretty face in contrast, and short, shiny, raven hair, was pushing the neatly arranged chairs in haphazard directions. I winced at the scraping sound the chairs made as they were dragged across the newly polished floorboards.

"Excuse me," I said, approaching the pretty young woman in the chic black pantsuit, who was sliding the chairs around. "I'm Mrs. Penelope Thornton-McClure, the co-owner of this store."

The young woman stopped pushing and smiled at me. Well, at least her mouth did. As far as I could tell, no *other* discernible facial tendon had been enlisted for the exercise.

"Hello, there," she said, "I'm Shelby Cabot from Salient House."

I had lived and worked in New York long enough to spot — from at least five paces — that plastic, time-to-handle-the-*non*-New-Yorker (i.e., simpleton) expression.

I extended my hand.

"Get those chairs rearranged, Shelby!" Brennan shouted. "These idiots gave me nothing but a blank wall and a rest room exit for a backdrop!"

Shelby shrugged, then turned away from me without a backward glance.

"Mr. Brennan," I said, dropping my unshaken hand, "perhaps I can help. I'm the co-owner of Buy the Book."

"Oh, yeah? So you're the one to blame, then? Didn't you even take the trouble to learn anything about how I like my appearances set up? We've got to turn this whole room forty-five degrees to the right. Get my back to those bookshelves over there. And put *my* novels *on* that bookshelf. Where's your brain? In your backside?"

"I'm so sorry, Mr. Brennan," I said, praying the sudden heat on my cheeks didn't come with the usual accompanying scarlet flush. (*Feeling* humiliated was one thing, but having one's own coloring announce it to the world was beyond excruciating.) "I didn't realize that your talk was being taped for television, or that you'd require a special arrangement of the space."

The *truth* was, George Young, the beloved and knowledgeable sales rep for Salient House who was based in Boston but handled all the independent bookstore orders for the state of Rhode Island, had gone off on a well-earned cruise vacation. Before he left, George advised us to call Salient House directly and ask for Shelby Cabot, the manager handling the publicity tour for Brennan.

I'd called, all right. Not once. Not twice. But *six* times. Six times I'd left messages in an effort to get the correct information. *Nobody,* not Shelby or anyone else, bothered to return my calls. I wanted to scream all of this back at Brennan, I really did, but I knew Brennan would find a way to turn things around and claim I was simply trying to get Shelby into trouble. Believe me, I'd encountered this sort of unfortunate blame game countless times while working in New York City publishing. There was no winning it.

"I'm so sorry," I mumbled again, feeling like the wimp of the century.

"You should be," said Brennan. "This place is a mess, but my daughter Deirdre and her husband, Kenneth, over there know how to fix it. They've done this many times before."

Another folding chair crashed to the floor. Kenneth, who was moving the refreshment table, almost tripped over it.

"God, Deirdre, your husband's such a klutz!" Brennan barked, kicking the chair out of the way.

I tried not to wince as I lifted the chair and set it upright. I turned to see what else needed to be righted when I noticed Deirdre glaring daggers at her father's back. Her husband, Kenneth, looked ready to strangle him.

I braced for the blowup. But none came. Deirdre's and Kenneth's features simply contorted, then relaxed again, as if enduring such assaults was a regular occurrence, as if giving in had become a habit.

As I already mentioned, I'd gone through the same thing back in New York — not just in my job but also in my marriage. Some battles you'd already fought and lost so many times that it suddenly seemed a waste of energy to even try fighting anymore.

Someone took my arm. I saw it was Shelby. She patted it and pulled me away, steering me toward the main bookstore as she quietly said, "Don't you worry now. Let me handle it. *I'm* a publishing professional."

"I've got it, Shelby!" A fresh-faced young man in khaki pants and a blue blazer rushed up to us brandishing a small paper bag.

"Good, Josh. Heel, boy," said Shelby. Josh narrowed his eyes at the polished publicity manager but said nothing.

Snatching the bag, Shelby reached inside and brought out a bottle filled with green liquid. "Thank God you got the right brand."

"What is that?" I asked, curious.

"Throat spray," said Shelby.

"Brennan won't speak without it," said Josh.

"That's fine, Josh," said Shelby through gritted teeth. "Now be a good boy and help us get this room fixed the way it *should* be."

"What way is *that,* pray tell?" asked Josh, batting his eyes and smirking.

"Okay to come in now?" called a man's voice.

Curious customers started wandering through the archway from the main store area. I rushed forward, embarrassed by the chaos of fallen chairs, a messed-up refreshment table, and a still-irate Timothy Brennan.

"Everything's all right, folks," I announced, shooing them back into the store area. "We'll have the room ready in a jiffy."

Glancing back, I saw Deirdre, Kenneth, Shelby, and Josh gathering up the fallen water bottles while Timothy Brennan told the technicians from the C-SPAN cable network how to do their jobs.

Chapter 3

A Postmortem Post

I don't want to achieve immortality
through my work. I want to achieve it
through not dying.

— Woody Allen

If there was a hell, Jack Shepard was in it.
Or else the universe was playing the cosmic
joke of the century. Why else would it doom
a guy like him to a place like this?

In life, Jack's blood had pulsed to the
rhythm of the city's streets. The smoky dice
joints and swingin' suds clubs, the back alleys, panel pads, and flophouses. The grifters
and grinders, Joe-belows and triggermen,
high rollers and sweet honeys — he knew
them all.

He even got to know the uptown joints
doing swing shifts as a bodyguard for cliff
dwellers — those high-rise society types. Believe it or don't, every third dame would get
all hopped up, take him back to her posh
Park Avenue pad, and jump his bones. *"What
do you say, big guy? Be my sixty-minute man?"*

Why couldn't eternity be a joint like *that*?

Instead, he got lead poisoning in the god-forsaken sticks — eternity in cornpone alley.

Now the only excitement Jack ever got was scaring the crap out of small-town operators witless enough to invade his cave. And when that bored him — as it always did — he'd *really* scare them, running them the hell out of his space.

At times, whole years would go by with blessed peace and quiet. And Jack found, when human activity was sparse, he could get some true rest settling into a sweet, forgetful limbo, a cosmic sleep akin to passing out after a bender.

He'd been in precisely that state when the damn construction had started. Hammering, sanding, painting, sawing . . . a lousy, nerve-racking racket in the lousy bookshop where somebody had punched his last ticket and given him the big chill.

Sure, Jack had played some pranks on the construction crew — making them think work tools had disappeared, sending energy surges through the electrical wiring — but they'd finished anyway.

Then that buggy dame had started in with the folding chairs. He'd watched her arrange them, one by one.

Unfold the chair.

Place the chair.

Adjust the chair.

Unfold another chair.

*R*eadjust the first chair.

Make a row.

Adjust the row.

Make another row.

If he'd been alive, Jack would have beat his own head against the stone wall until he'd blacked himself out. Instead, he'd made every chair appear turned on its damned head.

He had to give the broad credit, though. She hadn't screamed. Hadn't even made a peep, just hightailed it outta there, returning within minutes to see them set upright again.

Her name was Mrs. Penelope Thornton-McClure. And he had to admit she showed more moxie than a lot of grown *men* he'd pranked in the past fifty years.

Not a bad looker, either.

Had a nice face and soft voice. Certainly, she was the first living entity he'd even considered shifting himself toward since he'd crossed over, which was hilarious because, if he'd read her thoughts right, she didn't even believe in ghosts.

Well, he hadn't believed in them, either.

Concrete Jack. That's what he'd been. "I'm the hardest case you'll ever meet," he once told a client who wanted help beating a murder rap. "Too many con artists to count in this world. You want me to believe something, I gotta see proof. Show it to me plain as the broken nose on my face."

Just like Mrs. McClure, Jack had once be-

45

lieved that when you died, you died, and that was the end.

Brother, had he been wrong.

So he sat back and watched.

And right now, it was that broad, Penelope, he couldn't stop watching. Despite her sweet-as-pie face and her hard-work ethic, this Penelope doll could be pretty damned annoying. The chair-fixing compulsion was just one case in point. Still, the dame didn't deserve the crap she was getting from the biggest a-hole of the twentieth century if ever there was one —

Timothy Brennan.

Timothy Brennan, the lousy rat fink.

Before Brennan appeared, Jack had been observing the bookshop activities this evening with mild interest at best.

Now Jack was awake.

And alert.

And pissed.

Brennan didn't know it yet, but he'd just made the biggest mistake of his life: he'd finally walked into Jack's bookstore.

Chapter 4

A Drink before Dying

I'm just not sure we need this . . . mess
right now.
— Angie Gennaro to Patrick Kenzie, *Gone
Baby Gone* by Dennis Lehane, 1998

I was standing next to the refreshment table.
It had been dragged, on Brennan's orders, to
the back end of the room — unappealingly
close, in my opinion, to the rest rooms. Before me, a surreal sea of battered fedoras
bobbed with excitement. Murmurs of ap-
proval rose and fell amid the dark ties and
three-piece suits.

Timothy Brennan was leaning forward
against a carved oak podium (which I'd
bought for a song at a Newport estate sale),
captivating the crowd with his prepared
speech:

"Down these mean streets a man must go
who is not himself mean, who is neither tar-
nished nor afraid," Brennan read aloud.
"Such words could have been applied easily
to my fictional private detective, Jack Shield,
a man who was a complete man and a

common man, and above all a man of honor — by instinct, by inevitability, without thought of it, and certainly without saying it."

I winced.

Brennan had just asserted that "*Such words could have been applied easily to Jack Shield.*" But he'd somehow forgotten to mention that they were *Raymond Chandler's* exact words in his famous essay describing the quintessential detective.

I searched out Brainert, seated near the front. Not surprisingly, he was shaking his head with all the perfected disappointment of an English professor reviewing a badly footnoted paper. He caught my eye and together we mutely mouthed "Chandler. *The Simple Art of Murder.*"

I shrugged and lifted my hands palm up, as if to say, Perhaps it had been an innocent oversight.

Brainert rolled his eyes.

J. Brainert Parker (the J. was for Jarvis, a first name he'd utterly rejected since age six) was one of my closest childhood friends. A single, gay St. Francis College English professor in his thirties with a stringbean body, blanched complexion, and self-described "Ichabod Crane" style, he was also (as Sadie put it) one of those "relentlessly sober" types.

Brainert claimed to be a distant relative of

the Providence occult author H. P. Lovecraft; and, like his supposed ancestor, he was extremely well-read. All the regular customers respected his opinions. And his enthusiasm for out-of-print Holmes books kept the store's lights on — his most recent purchase being a forty-eight-dollar copy of a P. F. Collier & Son Holmes collection decorated red cloth hardcover, circa 1903.

In any event, I was feeling pretty badly about Brennan's unhappiness with our bookstore in general and me in particular. Before his speech, I'd actually tried to make peace by fetching him a cup of coffee and a plate of the Cooper Family Bakery goodies. The incoming guests were already digging into the food, and I was afraid Brennan wouldn't get to sample any of it.

Wrong. He'd practically slapped the five-nut tarts and Vermont maple doughnuts out of my hand, barking that he *never* ate anything before, during, or after his lectures.

"Are you running a bookstore or a diner?" he'd snapped at me. "*Water* only. Just *be sure* there's water."

Okay, I admit it: Timothy Brennan wasn't exactly the nicest author on the best-seller list. But I was willing to forgive his rudeness, his pomposity, his blustery impatience, even his quoting of Chandler without mentioning Chandler. Why? Because I myself was a huge fan of his books, purple prose and all. Maybe it was because Jack Shield could always say the sorts of things I wouldn't. Do the sorts of things I couldn't.

Whatever the reason, I enjoyed the Shield yarns as much as those old hard-boiled detective tales in the pulps of the twenties and thirties that my father had collected. Brennan himself hadn't been published in *Black Mask* (the magazine that had launched writers such as Raymond Chandler and Dashiell Hammett), but he'd known some of the men who had, and he wrote in their tradition. That was good enough for me. So like a pathetic kid defending some sports hero caught strung out on steroids, a part of me was still looking for excuses to defend the bad-behaving Brennan.

"It was back when I was a wet-behind-the-ears reporter that I first met and then knocked around with Jack Shepard," Brennan continued to tell the audience. "The model for my fictional detective was a tough-talking, no-nonsense, street-smart private eye dedicated to uncovering the truth, no matter where it leads."

Some members of the audience actually mouthed these familiar words right along with Brennan. They'd been part of the jacket copy for decades. Hoots and applause followed.

"Jack Shepard left me his case files. Changing the names to protect the guilty, I used them as the basis for my stories —"

A deep voice interrupted: *You did what?! You "used" them for your stories? Then you stole them, you low-down, dirty grifter. No one "left" you those files.*

Every muscle in my body froze in mortification. Some man had just heckled this beloved author. At *my* store! Brennan would never forgive me! And the crowd would tear the place to pieces!

I waited for the typhoon to hit.

But it didn't.

Brennan simply continued his speech. Ignoring the heckler, the audience obviously followed Brennan's lead.

"Lately, readers have been asking me if the real Jack Shepard was the equal of fictional Jack Shield," said Brennan. "I tell them that truthfully Shields is Shepard with Timothy Brennan mixed in. Shepard wasn't exactly leading-man material, y'know."

Yeah. Right. Not like you, ya bloated, barstool raconteur!

Once more, I braced for impact. *Surely* there would be a reaction this time. . . .

But Brennan disregarded the man — and so did his audience.

I scanned the crowded room, desperate to locate this deep-voiced pest. He sounded very close. But the only people standing near me, in front of the refreshment table, were women — Linda Cooper-Logan and Fiona

51

Finch, the sixty-year-old owner of Finch's Inn, the only hotel in Quindicott.

"Shepard had a ton of weaknesses and sad problems —"

Oh, and you didn't, ya degenerate, gambling ginhead!

What in *heaven's name* is going on? I thought. Was I the only one *hearing* this?

"And, frankly, he wasn't that smart," continued Brennan. "It took me — my writing, my words, and my ingenuity — to make him a hero that would span nineteen best-sellers and inspire two television shows. You might say I'm responsible for adding the heroism to the antihero."

No, Tim-bo. Sounds to me like you're responsible for stealing my stories, my life, and making a mint on it!

With a nauseating abruptness, I knew why no one else was reacting to the voice. And why I was the only one hearing it.

That voice wasn't in the room; it was inside my own head.

But how can that be? *How?* I asked myself. It wasn't *my* voice. Or my thoughts. I'd never thought such crude things in my entire life!

Of course you haven't, said the male voice. *You're one of those nice-thinking, fair-play Janes — gullible as a corn-fed calf and just about as defenseless.*

"Where are you?" I rasped in a loud whisper, unable to understand how the man

52

had answered me when I hadn't spoken a word.

Linda and Fiona looked at me with puzzled expressions.

"Where's who?" asked Linda.

I shook my head. "Forget it," I whispered.

"Jack Shepard and I were both working the mean streets," Brennan continued. "Jack as a detective and me as a reporter. We were just regular guys walking a thin line between the world of respectability and the underworld of crime."

HA!

I inhaled. Then exhaled. Joan of Arc heard voices, right? But they were probably nice, gentle, inspirational voices. Saintly voices.

I was the one walkin' that thin line, ya drunken bum. You were the one rackin' up debts at the track, bangin' poor workin' girls then callin' the cops on them to get out of payin', and drownin' your tonsils in so much suds I'd have to pick you up off the taproom floor.

I closed my eyes and opened them again. This voice was certainly no saint. And it *really* wasn't mine — at least not a voice from my *conscious* self. This left me with one conclusion: I was cracking up.

Get a grip, Penelope, I told myself. Refocus your attention!

As applause echoed off the walls, I concentrated on the crowd, scanning the mix of Quindicott townies, Providence professionals, and college kids, as well as Newport yacht-club and old-money types. All appeared entertained enough to shell out $27.50 each.

Then came the "no sale."

Unlike every other enraptured member of the audience, the middle-aged blond standing at the back of the room in a cream-colored cashmere sweater with white fox trim appeared to be suffering through the speech, her delicate features sculpted into an anguished grimace.

I remembered she'd arrived late and brushed me off when I'd offered to find her a seat, asking instead for the rest room. Her face actually seemed familiar. Suddenly I placed it:

Anna Worth, the Newport cereal heiress.

Worth Flakes and Nuts had been the family's claim to fame — it tasted somewhat like Wheaties but had nuts and dried fruit mixed in. Years ago she'd been involved in a scandal — typical eighties nightlife stuff, as I recalled, with shots fired at a boyfriend, a big publicized trial, and drug use afterward. It was odd to see her here in our little store, I thought — and not enjoying Brennan's talk very much, either, from the look on her face.

"Folks always ask me what happened to Jack Shepard," Brennan continued, "and I always had my stock answer: Jack Shepard let his weaknesses and, sorry to say, his stupidity get the better of him —"

54

Why you stinkin', stealin' son of a bitch! shouted the voice. *The only thing that got the better of me was you — if you're tellin' me you swiped my case files instead of gettin' off your lazy ass to look for me!*

(Clearly, refocusing my attention hadn't helped.)

"But it's finally time to reveal the truth," continued Brennan. Then he paused, taking time to look meaningfully into the camera. The audience seemed to collectively lean forward.

"In 1949, while Jack Shepard was working the case of a murdered army buddy, he vanished without a trace. Not even his body was found. For over fifty years now, I've wondered just what happened. Did the bad guys finally catch up with him? Did the corrupt authorities finally do Jack in? Or did someone set Jack up as a fall guy?"

Yeah, Tim-bo, ya smug-ass, tell them. I'd like to know myself.

"Shut up!" I rasped quietly to the voice in my mind, alarmed that I was losing my grip on reality. "Shut up! Shut up!"

Both Linda and Fiona again eyed me with concern. A few nearby guests even turned in their seats to deliver annoyed looks.

I felt the heat on my cheeks for the second time that night.

"Pen, are you okay?" Linda whispered. "Do you want to sit down?"

I shook my head.

"These questions will be answered in my *next* book," Brennan said. "And my first *non*fiction book. Ironic for an old reporter, eh? But the truth is" — Brennan paused to clear his throat — "for several years now I have been quietly investigating Jack's final case and his mysterious disappearance, and the solution to the fifty-plus-years mystery is close to being solved."

The audience clapped wildly. Brennan waved them down.

"Though Salient House and my fans have been clamoring for more Jack Shield mysteries, I am here to announce that *Shield of Justice* will be the very last *novel* of the series."

Disappointed murmurs sounded. Brennan's handsome son-in-law Kenneth rose from his seat in the front row and left the room. In the next seat, his well-dressed wife, Deirdre, watched him go with a clear look of distress on her plain face.

"It's finally time to find out . . ."

As Brennan cleared his throat again, he pulled the throat spray Josh had bought and spritzed it into his mouth.

"It's finally time to find out . . ."

Again he cleared his throat, and I realized with a start that what he really needed was some water. I reached behind me and let my fingers close on a plastic bottle resting on the refreshment table. With a quick twist, I unscrewed the cap, then stepped forward and set the bottle on the podium.

"About time," Brennan griped low before I returned to my spot.

"As I was saying, it's time to find out what happened to Jack Shepard and why, and to share that information with the world. My preliminary investigation shows that Jack Shepard's movements in the final days before his disappearance led him to a rare-book shop right here in Quindicott. Yes. The last place Jack Shepard visited in 1949 was *this* very store!"

As outcries of delighted surprise rippled through the audience, I decided I was probably the *most* shocked person in the entire room. My eyes found Aunt Sadie, who was standing just inside the archway that led to the other side of the bookstore. She simply shrugged, as if she had no idea what all this was about.

Timothy Brennan seemed pleased with the reaction and took a long pause to chug the entire contents of the Sutter Spring water bottle. Then he opened his mouth to speak again. Suddenly his eyes bulged and his face grew very flushed. His lips moved, but only a hoarse croak emerged. The water bottle dropped from his stubby fingers, and Brennan reached up to clutch his throat.

I watched, horrified, as his jowly face

turned scarlet, then paled.

"Mr. Brennan? What's wrong?" cried someone seated close to him.

He pointed to his throat, then reached out to grasp the podium, as if to steady himself. But a moment later, both man and podium tumbled to the floor.

"Call a doctor!" someone shouted.

I pushed through the throng of panicked people, looked down, and saw Timothy Brennan, his face chalk, his mouth opening and closing as rapidly as it had all evening, but this time without sound, just a terrible rhythmic sucking noise like a plunger desperately trying to pull something out of a blocked drain.

"Get back, please!" I cried. "Give him room!"

The sea of gray suits and battered fedoras backed away to give the flailing author room. All except Shelby Cabot of Salient House and his daughter Deirdre in her burgundy suit. They both knelt over the gasping man, their expressions grim. Josh stood back, behind Shelby, watching with equally grim concern. Deirdre took Brennan's hand.

The man's features relaxed, and his chest rose as he took a deep breath. His color began to come back. Then his eyes fluttered open.

"I think he's coming around," said Deirdre.

Brennan's eyes seemed to focus on the

person standing right next to me — Milner Logan. With a terrified gasp, Brennan raised his hand, frantically waving it as if warding away some evil spirit.

"Jack!" rasped Brennan, staring right up at Milner, who was now clutching his fedora in a white-knuckled grip. "J-J-Jack Shepard. It c-c-can't be. You're dead. You're dead!"

That's when Brennan's eyes closed. His face turned as gray as the fieldstone walls, and his rib cage collapsed with his last living breath.

Chapter 5

Hard-Boiled Bogey Man

The guy was dead as hell.
— Mike Hammer in *Vengeance Is Mine!*
by Mickey Spillane, 1950

"Pen? Penelope? Can you hear me?"

"She just drank too much, Sadie. Let her sleep it off down here."

"Okay, Milner. I'll walk you and Linda out."

I heard the voices, tried to open my eyelids, but for some reason they seemed to weigh more than a pair of unedited Stephen King manuscripts. "We gave him the heart attack," I murmured. "Half the audience . . . costumed like Jack Shepard . . . Oh, god . . . we killed him."

"Oh, no, she's starting *that* up again."

"It's too bad what happened, Sadie."

"Forget it," said Sadie. "Fate's fate. When your number's up, it's up. But thanks again for those baked goods. The crowd certainly devoured them."

"More of a wake than a party."

"So it was. But Brennan didn't go anywhere we're all not headed."

"True, Sadie. Good night."

" 'Night, Milner. 'Night, Linda . . ."

My pounding head lolled from side to side as I wrestled with dreamland. When consciousness finally won, I rose from the rocking chair and moved shakily through the dimly lit store.

"Anyone here?"

My mouth was cotton. I checked my watch. Big hand on twelve, little on four.

Well, the party's certainly over, I thought, looking at our beautifully renovated store, all the new inventory, the antiques, the fixtures. All our hopes and efforts . . .

More than the party was over, and I knew it.

Timothy Brennan had been Buy the Book's very first author appearance, and he'd ended up dead. Talk about cursed. Now authors would avoid our store in droves — right along with the customers. Not that they hadn't before. This incident just gave them a new reason.

I sighed. Who in the world would patronize us now?

Maybe Brennan's ghost, I thought. If I believed in ghosts.

Brainert once said that ghosts in stories meant unfinished business. But he'd been talking about literary devices.

As my shaky legs moved beneath the archway that led to the community events space, I tried to recall the last time I'd considered actual spirits. It had been years. Back when I'd watched them lower my mother into the muddy earth of the Quindicott Village Cemetery.

At the ripe old age of thirteen, I had been certain that death was not the end. Every night I'd whisper into the dark from beneath my blanket. I'd tell my mother about my day at school, a boy I liked, a grade I got. I was certain my mom could hear, just couldn't answer. Not in a normal way but in signs.

I had looked for signs of my mother everywhere, and I'd found them. In the shape of a cloud, or a piece of music on the radio. In the way a bird would follow me home or a phrase some stranger might utter on the street.

After school every day, rain or shine or snow, I used to visit my mother's grave at the old Q cemetery, bring her a flower, read her a poem. Sometimes I'd visit other graves, too. A neighbor boy who'd been hit by a car. A favorite teacher who'd suffered a massive heart attack. A teenage girl who'd drowned.

I'd become an expert at talking to the dead. And, a few times, when I'd been under great stress at school, I even thought I could hear the dead speaking to me. A voice here or there.

But then I lost my older brother. And my dad.

At seventeen, I suddenly stopped looking for signs. Or visiting graves to talk to the dead. It seemed pointless: I was alive, and they were not. Wherever they'd gone, they'd left me behind. And it suddenly seemed clear that the only thing the dead left the living was *alone*. So that was that.

One of the store's dim night-lights shone in the corner. The chairs had been folded up and stacked against the far wall, leaving a wide expanse of empty floor. No police tape or chalk lines or anything out of the ordinary. Why should there be? Brennan died of natural causes — a heart attack, perhaps. Or a stroke. I deliberately chose not to think about the other possibility: fright! *No*, I told myself, *we didn't frighten Timothy Brennan to death, despite his puzzling last words.*

Sadly, I saw that the refreshment table was empty. Totally clean. No goodies, no soda, no bottled water. I sighed. My mouth felt as dry as the Sahara desert. No doubt from the whiskey. I could use a stiff drink of something wholesome and nonalcoholic, preferably bottled water.

I gazed at the carved oak podium, now standing in the corner, the spot where Brennan had fallen. A doctor in the audience had performed CPR on the author for ten minutes before the paramedics finally arrived to pronounce him done for. There would be no ghost.

"When you're dead you're dead and that's all there is," I mumbled.

Oh, yeah? Who says so?

I froze.

No, I thought. No way. I couldn't be hearing the very same deep male voice that had heckled Brennan's speech.

I took a step back, searched. But there was no one. Still, the room was too dark to see through every shadow.

"Whoever you are, the party's over, okay?" I said, trying and failing to sound commanding. "You have to leave now."

Believe me, honey, I would if I could.

I told myself to keep steady. Sadie and Spencer were upstairs. I had to get this guy out. Now.

"What do you want? Money? I doubt we sold many books today."

Think again, doll. You sold them all.

"What?"

They're all gone. Look for yourself.

I wanted to run full speed to the back room, but I hesitated. What if this man were hiding in the corner shadows? What if he were luring me into a trap?

No trap. Go look.

"How did you know what I was thinking?"

Don't know how. Just do.

I went back to the main part of the store,

reached under the counter where the register sat, and let my fingers close on Sadie's aluminum baseball bat. Sadie would have locked up the money in the safe upstairs, so the back room was the only evidence.

As I drew the bat out, I knocked over a half-filled bottle of water. After Brennan had collapsed, I remembered grabbing it off the table as a pacifier, drinking half the contents, then stashing it here during the craziness of the ambulance and police coming in.

I was dying of thirst, so I unscrewed the cap, took a swig from the bottle, put the cap back on, and started for the community events space again, the bottle tucked under one arm and the bat raised high.

"Stay out of my way if you don't want a bashed-in skull," I said.

Too late, said the man.

I flipped the main switch. Dozens of bulbs sparked to life in the newly installed track system. The entire space brightened and revealed . . . no one.

I moved toward the exit to the rest room and the back room area, swiping at switches the whole way. When I got to the chilly, bare storage room, I almost dropped the bat.

In the corner were more than a dozen crushed cardboard boxes. Not one was left unravaged.

"Three hundred hardcovers," I murmured, doing the math in my head. "That's twenty-seven fifty a copy times three hundred . . . forty-six percent of which we keep. That's almost four thousand dollars. In one night!"

An average annual income in my time. Good haul, honey.

I wheeled, searching for the man who kept speaking. But there was no one. "Where in hell are you!"

Right here. With you.

I couldn't take it. I ran from the storage area, bat *still* in hand.

"I'm calling the police!"

To tell them what? You're hearing voices?

My steps slowed. I looked around again. He wasn't wrong. I couldn't see him. What was I going to tell the cops? An invisible man was talking to me. The Quindicott police would have trouble finding a criminal who walked up to their front door!

(It wasn't their fault, really. They had little resources and even less experience with anything close to a felony. Mostly they broke up fights at the high school football games and gave out speeding tickets to those high-priced performance cars on their way to Newport or Cape Cod.)

"What's your name?" I demanded, hoping I could just talk him out of hiding.

Name's Jack.

"Jack what?"

Jack Shepard.

"That's not funny." .

I'm not trying to be funny.

"No, you're trying to scare me, and I don't appreciate it."

Well, ain't that a tragedy. At least you sold your books.

"Yes. True. That's good news. And you were right about it. But I'm sure it's just a one-night fluke."

Maybe. But I'll tell you what's not a fluke: Brennan's death.

"What do you mean?"

He was murdered, honey. Set up. And sent up.

My mouth still felt like an arid wasteland. I pulled the bottle from under my arm, unscrewed the cap, and drank again.

Don't choke now.

I lowered the bottle. "That's an awful thing to say."

Awww, take a break from Miss Priss-land, would ya?

"What?!"

You nice-thinking Janes really burn me up.

"Well, the same to you, whoever you are —"

I told you. Jack Shepard.

"Shut up! I've had just about enough. If you're such a big, tough, hard-boiled dick, then why are you hiding, huh? Where the heck are you? Too afraid to show yourself?" I moved slowly through the store, still seeing no one. I edged back toward the community events space.

There was a long pause. I tightened my

grip on the bat. Finally the deep voice spoke again.

Turn off the light.

Oh, shit, I thought.

Deep male laughter filled my head. *Thought you didn't use such language.*

"How could you hear that? I didn't say it."

Baby, I don't know how, but I can hear your thoughts. I just can. So? You want to see me? Turn OFF the lights.

This was just someone from the book-signing party, I told myself. Someone playing a game. I moved to the end of the room, where I felt I could dash away quickly if I didn't like what I saw.

I licked my lips nervously and took a final swig from the bottled water, draining it completely. It tasted good, I realized. There was a subtle flavor I couldn't place. For some reason it reminded me of one of Milner's pastries.

Had Sutter Spring started flavoring their water now?

The thought might have bothered me, but I had a more pressing consideration at the moment, so I put the bottle on the floor, positioned the bat in a defensive position, and flipped off the lights.

The dull glow of the recessed security lights were the only illumination. That and the silvery streaks from the streetlights beyond the big front window on this side of the store.

Bat at the ready, I scanned the room. Then I saw it: a shadow on the wall. A fedora on a square-jawed profile. Broad-suited shoulders tapering down to a narrow waist.

Whoever he was, he had obviously read my newspaper ads and come in costume.

The shadow moved, and I took a step back. I saw the figure's arm come up. One finger pushed at the brim of his fedora, moving it back on his head. Then he folded his arms over his broad chest. It was a confident gesture, masculine and sure.

I'm Jack Shepard, Mrs. McClure. Or to be absolutely precise — you like precision, don't you? I'm his ghost.

I watched the shadow move off the wall, watched as it became three dimensions and stepped like a dark figure through an invisible archway and into the room. Outside, headlights from a passing car shot shafts of silver through the window, and in the briefest moment of illumination, I glimpsed his visage plain as day: the sunken cheeks, the crooked nose, the iron jaw, and the one-inch scar in the shape of a dagger slashing across the flat, square chin.

Whoever he was, he held the same relentlessly masculine features of the man whose grimacing photo graced every one of Timothy Brennan's books.

"You can't be Jack Shepard. You *can't* be. He's *dead!*"

69

Now you're gettin' it.

My bat dropped to the floor. And about two seconds later, so did I.

Chapter 6

The Morning After

Publicity darling, just publicity. Any kind is better than none at all.
— Raymond Chandler, "Blackmailers Don't Shoot," *Black Mask*, December 1933 (Chandler's debut short story)

"Howya feeling, honey?"

First I heard the voice. Then the rattle and snap of a shade going north. The warmth of sunlight streaked across my face, and I lifted my thousand-pound eyelids. The silhouette of a heavy oak bookcase came into focus like the dark center of a blinding eclipse. I read the spines of dust jackets: Rendell, Rhode, Rice, Rinehart . . . Obviously, I was in the R's.

I turned to see Aunt Sadie's slight form bustling from the tall picture window to the store's front door, the streaming sun rays illuminating those "Shirley MacLaine highlights" in her short auburn hair. She was out of her dress and back in her preferred sort of outfit: gray slacks and a white T-shirt, over which she'd thrown a large unbuttoned, untucked denim shirt.

"How am I feeling?" I repeated. "Like a full floor display got dropped on my head from the top of the Empire State Building. I swear I'll never touch hard liquor again."

"Just sit tight, dear, I'll get you something to drink." She unlocked the door, then vanished, her four-foot-eleven frame dashing so fast across the polished plank floorboards it made my already spinning head spin even more.

" 'Something to drink,' " I muttered. "I don't know . . . seems to me I got *into* this state with that advice. . . ."

I was still wearing last night's outfit, less than presentable after a night tossing in a rocking chair: My black skirt was wrinkled, my pale blue sweater set felt grungy against my skin, my slingback heels had been kicked off — where? I had no clue — and my pantyhose displayed more than one run.

Suddenly Sadie was back. "Here," she said, handing me a steaming mug of coffee along with one of the Cooper Family Bakery's leftovers from the night before. "I managed to save a few of the carrot-cake muffins with cream cheese icing. They're your favorite, aren't they?"

"Okay," I said, "maybe life's worth living after all."

"Wasn't easy saving them, I can tell ya. That crowd was cooped up here for two hours giving their names and statements to

Welsh and Eddie. Seems like a lot of fuss over an unfortunate incident."

Officers Welsh Tibbet and Eddie Franzetti (of the Franzetti's Pizza Place Franzettis) were the two Quindicott cops who'd been sent to the bookstore after Brennan's death. Our town was large enough for a small police force but way too small to support anything more. For investigations, forensics, and the like, the old Q cops relied on the state. I figured taking names and statements was simply routine.

"Where's Spencer?" I asked.

"Upstairs, still sleeping. It was a late night for everyone." Sadie unlocked the front door but left the CLOSED sign in place since, mercifully, we weren't scheduled to open for another hour. Then she turned to me and grinned.

Now, why the heck is she so happy? I wondered. We'd just had our first author appearance — and the author hadn't survived it. And how the heck did my derriere get back into this rocking chair? I remembered passing out on the floor.

Well, if I woke up in this rocker, I reasoned, I must NOT have passed out on the floor, which pointed to one conclusion:

"I had a funny dream," I blurted, my mouth half full of muffin.

"You don't say," Sadie said. "Ha-ha funny or spooky-weird funny?"

"I talked to the ghost of Jack Shepard."

Sadie was quiet a long moment. "That'd be the spooky-weird kind then, wouldn't it?"

"You're telling me."

"What did he say to you, Pen?"

"Oh . . . I don't know. . . ." I ate more muffin, chewed, swallowed, and suddenly regretted saying anything. "It was just an outlandish dream. . . ."

"*What* did he tell you?" Sadie's voice wasn't kidding around. Her pine green eyes had focused in and locked on.

"He didn't say much," I hedged. "Just that we sold all of our Jack Shield books, for one thing. Isn't that crazy? I mean, nobody sells three hundred hardcovers out of a store this small in one night."

"We did."

"What?" I nearly dropped the hot mug of coffee into my skirt's wrinkled lap.

"We sold every last copy."

"HOW? There weren't three hundred people in the store last night!"

"No, but there were just over one hundred, and these were serious fans. Most bought multiple copies of *Shield of Justice* along with every last title in Timothy Brennan's backlist. There isn't one Jack Shield book left in the store."

"They bought multiple copies?"

"Darn right. Some bought four or five, just to have the sales receipt that showed the date

74

it was purchased — the day Brennan died — and to show where it was purchased."

"Where it was purchased," I repeated, distracted. For most bookstores, turnover of an initial print order took six to eight *weeks*, not one night.

"Yes, *where* it was purchased is now vital to these fans," said Sadie. "Before he died, Brennan announced he'd traced Shepard's last movements in '49 to *this* very store. *Our store!*"

"Right. I remember. It still sounds crazy, though."

"Hey," Sadie suddenly called from the archway connecting the main store with the events space, "what's my baseball bat doing on the floor?"

I rose so fast from my cross-hatched Shaker seat, I set my head to rocking more violently than the chair. In stockinged feet I managed to stumble over to the archway without landing on my face, although I did end up shredding the last vestiges of nylon covering my toes.

Sadie pointed to the aluminum bat. It rested on the wood plank floor in the exact spot where I'd been talking to the ghost — before I blacked out, that is. My slingbacks were here, too.

"I think . . . I must have been . . . sleep-walking," I concluded.

"Part of your ghost dream?" asked Sadie,

picking up the bat.

"Yes," I said, slipping back into my shoes. "Let's just drop it, okay?"

I stuffed the last bit of muffin into my mouth — hoping to swallow my anxieties along with it. Then I drained my coffee mug and headed toward the stairs, intending to check on Spencer, shower, change, and stuff at least one more delicious muffin in (my size fourteen skirt was already tight, but after the night I had, I figured I deserved a little baked-good comfort). That's when the bell above the front door tinkled and a female voice sharply called out:

"Sadie Thornton!"

Completely ignoring the CLOSED sign, town councilwoman Marjorie Binder-Smith barreled through our front door, wearing one of her numerous pink suits.

"Now, what in hell could *she* want?" muttered Sadie.

"Have you seen the morning paper?" Marjorie waved a copy of the Saturday morning *Quindicott Bulletin* in front of our faces and commanded, "Just take a look at this!"

We did. The headline, which stretched the width of the front page in letters at least two inches tall, stated: *Noted Author Dies in Local Bookstore Mishap!*

"Please tell me, ladies," said the councilwoman, "*why* someone choked to death on a doughnut in a business that does *not* have a license to sell food?"

"Choked to death? On a doughnut?" I repeated. I skimmed the story. The general news was correct, but some of the details were all wrong.

"Well, what have you got to say for yourself?" demanded the sixtyish councilwoman. Her voice sounded outraged, but her eyes, edged by the cracks that came from applying a copious amount of face powder, held the glee of a driller making an oil strike — a timely issue to exploit was just the thing to raise a politico's profile.

I was about to answer her charge when Aunt Sadie put herself between us.

"Calm down, Marjorie," she said. "You don't want to pop any plastic surgery stitches, do you?"

Ha! Hahahahahaha!

The laughter in my ears was deep and loud. The laugh of Jack Shepard. I looked immediately for a reaction from Sadie or Marjorie, but neither appeared to have heard it.

"You can't be real," I silently told the Jack Shepard voice. "I dreamed you up. That's all you are. A delusion."

Think again, babe, said the deep voice. *I've been here since before you were born.*

"Be quiet now," I silently told the voice. "I can't deal with this delusion on top of everything else!"

The councilwoman was now shaking her finger in Sadie's face. "Don't you threaten me, Sadie Thornton!"

"Threat?" Sadie said calmly. "That was no *threat*. Really, Marjorie, can't you recognize a simple *insult* when you hear it?"

I so hated confrontations. But whenever Sadie and Marjorie were in a room together, friction seemed inevitable. Sadie would never discuss the reason, but the bad blood between the two women was long-standing. It predated even the feud between Marjorie and the Quindicott small-business owners, which had been going strong for well over a decade.

Linda Cooper-Logan had actually dubbed the woman "the Municipal Zoning Witch" because of the relentless list of regulations and taxes she continually attempted to pass on local businesses.

The woman had very wealthy backers, too, thanks in part to her willingness to advance their private concerns. The McClures were among them. They still owned quite a bit of land in Quindicott, despite the fact that most of their residences were in New York, Palm Beach, and Newport.

In return for her various "favors," to people such as the McClures, Marjorie expected backing for the Council president's office next year and maybe even the governor's office in the future — or so she liked to tell people. Lately, she'd taken to wearing Hillary

Clinton pastel suits, and, according to Colleen, she'd even asked for her brown hair to be dyed blond and cut short à la Hillary.

"Hillary Smillary," Aunt Sadie had said when Colleen had passed along the gossip. "Thirty years ago that woman was obsessed with the Kennedys. Even dyed her hair black like Jackie O's. Marjorie is just a silly, silly woman."

"I know your tactics, Marjorie," said Sadie, tightening her grip on the aluminum bat and raising it up just a fraction from her side. "You're always looking for some issue to advance your political profile. Well, you're not latching onto this one — even if it *is* the biggest news that's hit this town since Seymour Tarnish won twenty-five thousand dollars on *Jeopardy!*"

"You're wrong, Sadie." Marjorie's eyes narrowed and she actually poked her manicured finger into Sadie's small shoulder. "This isn't about politics, it's about rules. You haven't paid the town for the proper license to sell food!"

What a shakedown artist, said the Jack Shepard voice. *You want some advice? Grab that bat and give it a swing or two.*

"Shut up," I rasped.

"What did you tell me?" said Marjorie, wheeling to confront me.

"Take it easy," I said, quickly backing up a step. "We don't have a license to sell food

79

because we aren't *selling* food. You can check with the people who came last night. Welsh and Eddie took down all their statements —"

"You're denying you had food here? What about the doughnut Brennan choked on, then?"

"We did serve complimentary refreshments during the social gathering, which is within our right," I said. "But Timothy Brennan didn't choke to death on a doughnut. He didn't even eat."

"What about the news report?" challenged Marjorie, slapping at the paper in my hand.

"It's the *Quindicott Bulletin*, not the *Boston Globe*!" cried Sadie. "It's Elmer Crabtree, for cripes sake!"

Elmer, the *Quindicott Bulletin*'s publisher, was pushing eighty these days, but his age wasn't the issue. His primary business had always been as local printer of things such as supermarket flyers, sales brochures, and wedding invitations. More than forty years ago, he'd started the *Bulletin* not to extend the fourth estate or to put truth on the kitchen tables of the Quindicott citizenry, but to make a tidy profit from local business ads and grocery store coupons.

The *Bulletin*'s contents, therefore, mostly consisted of verbatim press releases from town officials, notices for local meetings, sports scores from school teams, and classified ads for selling used cars and the like. He wrote up the occasional "hard news" story on his front page — like the piece on Brennan's death. But he was almost never an eyewitness — and neither were his usual sources. The accounts, in fact, were primarily told to him third- and fourthhand.

"You know how he gets most of his news?" said Sadie. "Busybodies leaving messages on his phone machine!"

"It doesn't matter if it's true. It's in print!" cried Marjorie.

"I can understand your concern," I said quickly, trying to defuse the argument. "But even Brennan's own daughter Deirdre can verify he ate nothing. In fact, Brennan told me he never eats at author appearances — he probably had a nervous stomach or something."

"Well, if he didn't choke on a doughnut, what did he *die* of, then?" asked Marjorie.

"His daughter mentioned in passing that he had a weak heart." I was reaching — my nervous shrug making *that* patently obvious. "But I'm sure the state medical examiner's autopsy results will be made public."

Then I thought about all those fans dressed as Jack Shield and the terrified look on Brennan's pale face before he died. My stomach nearly lost its contents. Of course, I kept as brave a face as possible in front of the councilwoman. My bright idea may have inadvertently helped along Brennan's heart attack, but Buy the Book certainly hadn't done anything criminal.

"Well, I'm warning you both right now that I've already made a few phone calls to the proper authorities," said the councilwoman, turning her pink leather pumps toward the door. "And no matter what the outcome of their investigation, it's more than apparent you've brought bad luck to this town — and most likely busted our budget, too. I shudder to think of the municipal overtime costs incurred from last night's . . . *mishap*."

After a martyr's sigh, she continued, "I tell you, I've been working for years to bring business back to Quindicott, and this botched event is sure to set the economic clock backward. I swear, if you've ruined this town's chances for a recovery, I'll come after your license to operate a business at all!"

Marjorie opened her mouth, about to continue, when she stopped abruptly, her eyes taking in my disheveled appearance, from my shredded hosiery to my copper tangles. "Penelope Thornton-McClure, what in the world *happened* to you? You look as though you've been out partying all night! What sort of life have you got your son involved in? I just spoke to your sister-in-law, and I'm sure the McClures would not approve."

Here we go, I thought.

After Calvin's leap, the McClures — led primarily by Calvin's older sister, Ashley

McClure-Sutherland — never came right out and *said* they blamed me for Calvin's suicide; that maybe *I* was the crazy one; and that my son would be better off with them than me. But I knew very well they were constantly looking for an excuse to take my boy away.

"Aw, get lost, already," Sadie told Marjorie.

"Fine," she said, "I'm going. But I *must* remind Penelope that the McClures are expecting to see her and Spencer at Gardener's big birthday party tomorrow. The precious boy is turning nine. It's a very big day, you know. I'm invited as well, of course."

"Marjorie, I'm sorry, but I told my sister-in-law already, Spence and I can't make it. Sadie and I just reopened the store a week ago, and I need to be here to work."

"Yes, well, Ashley said you might be too busy, with this store and all. That's why she told me to tell you she's going to have her chauffeur pick up Spencer and drive him to the Newport estate. Spencer has a right to see his cousin, you must admit."

"I don't think Spence should go without me —" I began, but Marjorie cut me off.

"Nonsense!" said Marjorie. With one more snide look, she added, "You don't want me to suggest to them that I found you looking as though you'd been out partying all night . . . do you?"

Tell her to go to hell, the ghost voice said in my head.

83

I gritted my teeth and ignored it.

"The car will be here at nine o'clock sharp. Make sure he's ready. Ta!" With a wave of her hand and a tinkling of the door's little bell, Marjorie was gone. Sadie looked mad enough to spit. But she didn't have time.

The door's Tinkerbell impersonation started up again, followed by a loud "Hi-yooooooo!"

Vinny Nardini, our Dependable Delivery Service man, strode in with clipboard in hand and the old *Tonight Show* Ed McMahon greeting. A gentle guy with bark-colored hair and a full beard, Vinny had been on the Quindicott High School football team with my late older brother, Pete, who'd died at age twenty while drag racing his souped-up GTO to impress MaryJo Lerrotta. Whenever I saw Vinny's large frame sporting the universally recognized DDS brown uniform, I couldn't help thinking of Peter.

If my brother had lived, I was certain he would have made close to the same choices as Vinny, who had taken a job in Quindicott, married a girl from Quindicott, and quickly begun to raise three children in Quindicott. Vin was pretty typical of most of the people with whom my brother and I had gone to school. He was also one of the happiest guys I knew.

"Hi-yo, yourself," said Sadie. "What are you doing here? We're not even open yet."

My aunt was as surprised as I was to see a DDS man on a Saturday.

"I'm collecting names. A petition to save the town square squirrels," he said, presenting his electronic clipboard to Sadie. "Sign here, young woman, to stock the city hall with nuts."

"I hope I'm not signing for a shipment of narcotics," said Sadie.

"I only deliver heroin on Thursdays," said Vinny.

Ha! Hahahahahaha!

The ghost voice. Again.

As Vinny went back out to his boxy brown DDS truck, the door tinkled yet again.

"Good morning, all," said Professor Brainert Parker. He was such an old friend, and good customer, ignoring the CLOSED sign had become routine.

On teaching days, Brainert always wore a three-piece suit and tie. Today, however, was "casual" weekend wear, which for Brainert expressed itself in a wrinkle-free yellow cotton buttoned-down tucked into pressed J. Crew khakis with a knife-sharp crease.

"Have you seen the *Bulletin*?" he asked.

Sadie rolled her eyes. I held up the offending front page.

"Elmer Crabtree strikes again," said Brainert.

The door swung wide once more, with Vinny pulling a handcart filled with cardboard boxes. He unloaded twenty in all. Five at a time. Each held twenty-five hardcover books. Sadie read the words stamped on the side of each box: "*Shield of Justice.*"

"This must be a mistake," I said in shock. "We already received this order!"

"No mistake," said Vinny, piling the last of the boxes up by the checkout counter. "And Sadie's signed, so it's off my hands — and my truck. Toodles."

"Oh, my goodness," I told Sadie. "I remember now. That Shelby woman from Salient House, the publicist, she cornered me right before Brennan spoke. She said she'd convinced Brennan to stay over a few days and come back to our shop to sign all weekend. She said she had the warehouse on her cell phone and needed the store's account number to approve an order of 'a few' more books. I agreed to 'a few,' not five hundred!"

"Hen's teeth," said Sadie.

"What do we do?" I said. "Brennan isn't about to rise from the dead to sign these now —"

I wouldn't make book on that.

Ohmygod.

"You're right. We'll never move this many copies," said Sadie. "After last night's run, I think we already must have sold a *Shield of Justice* book to every Jack Shield fan in a fifty-mile radius."

"Can't you just send back the unopened boxes to the publisher on Monday for credit? No harm done?" asked Brainert.

"Normally, yes," I said. "But Salient House just instituted a new penalty policy."

"Oh, dear. I'd forgotten," said Sadie.

To discourage returns, the publisher now made bookstores pay a penalty when returning more than 50 percent of any order. Plus postage.

"We'll still come out ahead," said Sadie.

"Yes, but it's a shame to lose *any* of the profit," I told her. "We need every penny —"

"Well, why don't we at least refill the display?" she suggested. "Who knows, we might move a few copies over the weekend."

We unpacked exactly one box of *Shield of Justice* and wheeled the remaining nineteen into the back, where I rubber-stamped them with the "Property of Buy the Book" seal. But I knew that designation was only temporary.

On Monday, the bulk of this shipment would surely go back to the publisher's warehouse under the most dreaded designation in the book trade — a ghastly, horrifying word no bookseller, publisher, or author ever wished to utter:

RETURNS.

Chapter 7

Crime Scene

Chandler began to wonder whether even hard-boiled murder stories were not going to seem "a bit on the insignificant side" . . . considering the publicity given to real-life urban homicide.
— Tom Hiney, *Raymond Chandler: A Biography*

As I returned from the storage room, I noticed a crowd gathering on the sidewalk.

Customers? Already?

Buy the Book wasn't supposed to open for another fifteen minutes or so, but now I considered opening early. I glanced briefly at the crowd and spied a familiar face: Josh, Shelby Cabot's assistant from Salient House. I assumed he'd come to pay a courtesy call on behalf of the publisher. "We're so sorry our author dropped dead on you and we stocked your business with an immovable ton of his unsigned books."

I was just calculating how many *Shield of Justice* cases he could haul back to New York City with him — thereby allowing us to dodge the penalty and postage — when the crowd spotted me at the door and began to surge forward. I reached to flip the CLOSED sign to OPEN when something slapped against the window and stayed there. A Rhode Island State Policeman had just announced his presence by smacking his gold badge against my window.

The door opened and I jumped backward. A huge figure loomed in the doorway. Massive shoulders blocked out the sun. I saw a square chin covered with blond stubble, a bull neck, icy-gray eyes, and that big gold badge.

Suddenly I felt queasy all over again.

"Excuse me, ma'am. My name is Detective-Lieutenant Roger Marsh of the Crime Investigation Unit of the State Police. I have a warrant to seal and search these premises and any indoor or outdoor space attached to this address —"

He dangled an official-looking document in front of me as a small bull-necked army of men — some in plainclothes, with silver metal attaché cases, and some wearing gray uniforms with red trim and Smokey the Bear hats — filed into my store.

"Why? Whatever could you want here?" Sadie demanded, rushing out of the stockroom. Lieutenant Marsh ignored her, his eyes fixed on me.

"— And to confiscate any and all materials

deemed relevant to the investigation," he continued.

"But —" I muttered.

Lieutenant Marsh's cold gray eyes shut me up. He studied me with such ferocity, I felt my cheeks burning with a sudden flush, realizing how disheveled I must have looked. Marsh noticed my discomfort immediately. I swear his eyes grew even more frosty.

"What investigation?" I asked, finally regaining the power of speech.

"The investigation into the events surrounding a suspicious death that occurred on these premises last evening," Lieutenant Marsh replied, his eyes never leaving mine.

"Suspicious death?" Brainert said with a snort. "Don't you mean 'mishap'?"

The lieutenant's eyes shifted to Brainert.

"Who are you, sir? And why are you here?"

I could see Brainert's thin chest swell as his face turned scarlet with indignation. I took a breath and waited for the explosion. But before it came, Officer Eddie Franzetti of the Quindicott Police hurried through the door and practically threw himself between the lieutenant and Brainert. Behind Eddie came four more officers of the State Police, and Eddie's partner, Officer Tibbet. Beyond them I could see the shocked and surprised faces of the crowd still waiting on the sidewalk to enter the store.

"I think you should leave now, *Professor*

Parker," Eddie said diplomatically as he took hold of Brainert's arm. "Let's give Lieutenant Marsh the space he needs to do his job."

"I . . . I . . ." Brainert stammered.

As graceful as a dancer, Eddie sent Brainert into his partner's arms, who led Brainert out the door. Then Officer Franzetti turned and faced us. "Detective-Lieutenant Marsh needs access to any foods or beverages left over from last night's event," he explained, looking at me. "And his forensics team will need to see where the garbage was dumped."

I stammered, unable to help Detective-Lieutenant Marsh for the simple reason that I was in an alcohol-induced slumber when the community events space was cleaned and the chairs folded. Fortunately, Aunt Sadie stepped in.

"There are some bottles of water in the storeroom," she said. "And the garbage from last night was thrown into the Dumpster in back."

Detective-Lieutenant Marsh nodded to his team, and two uniformed officers took off — presumably to the back to retrieve our suspicious garbage.

"Lock that door," Marsh barked.

"We're due to open —" Sadie said.

"Only when we're done here," Detective-Lieutenant Marsh said. "Not before. Right now these premises are considered a crime scene and are closed to the public until my forensics team gathers evidence and completes their initial investigation."

Aunt Sadie nodded.

The plainclothed detective turned and scanned the sidewalk. "Looks like death was good for business," Marsh said meaningfully. Then his eyes fixed on me once again.

"I will also need to interview" — he double-checked the warrant in his hand — "a Mrs. Penelope Thornton-McClure."

I nodded, getting more and more uncomfortable under the lieutenant's suspicious gaze.

"If you need to see the leftovers, just follow me," Sadie said. She turned and marched to the storeroom.

Marsh and the last of his uniformed Staties followed Aunt Sadie. When they were out of sight — and earshot — Eddie turned to me. We both let out sighs at the same time.

Officer Eddie Franzetti, the eldest son of Joe Franzetti, was one of my late brother's best friends back in high school. Though now a family man, he still retained his boyish charm. And he was quite handsome — especially so in his dark blue police uniform. Unlike his brothers, who were content to sling pizza dough at the family restaurant, Eddie wanted something different out of life. A stint in the military was followed by a job on the local police force — and marriage to the most popular girl in Quindicott High School. I always liked Eddie and knew I could trust him to be straight with me now.

"So what's going on?" I asked in a soft whisper.

Eddie tilted his hat back and scratched his head. "Apparently, Councilwoman Binder-Smith made a few phone calls last night after she heard what happened here. When the police chief was less than responsive to the councilwoman's 'suggestions' she went over his head."

"To the State Police!" I said. "She must have called in a lot of favors to get them involved."

"Not really. All it takes is a request from a town official — the mayor, the police, or a town councilman — to bring in the Staties," explained Eddie. "And if the circumstances require it, a warrant can be issued within minutes."

"Great. Thanks for the civics lesson."

I told myself it didn't matter. Once the autopsy came through — and it was officially established that Timothy Brennan's death was from natural causes — then all of this was sure to go away. But a voice inside told me that my troubles were only beginning. And another voice — not mine at all — said something I didn't want to hear:

Baby, sounds to me like you're a picture being fitted for a frame, and the name of that frame is murder.

I leaned against the counter, trying to catch my breath. I told myself to ignore the "ghost" voice and be reasonable, logical, practical.

"Brennan wasn't murdered," I silently told myself — and that annoying deep voice. "He died of some sort of stroke or heart attack. An autopsy will certainly prove it, and then all this . . . *mess* will go away."

Officer Franzetti was still speaking, but I just nodded at his words, not really hearing them.

Outside, I noticed the crowd swelling. Even on top of the other shocks of this morning, that surprised me. I thought the arrival of the State Police would have scared them off. Instead it seemed to attract even more curious people.

I searched the crowd for the face of Josh, the young man from Salient House. But he was gone — the only one the army of State Policemen seemed to scare, I noted.

"Eddie, excuse me," I suddenly said. "I need to go upstairs, see to my son, and clean up."

"Oh, sure, Pen. Take your time." His chin gestured toward the Staties at work. "I know *they* will."

Great. Just great, I thought. A record crowd at opening, and we're closed for an episode of *CSI*.

Chapter 8

Curious Jack

There are things happening. . . . They go on right under your very nose and you never know about them.
— Mike Hammer, *My Gun Is Quick* by Mickey Spillane, 1950

After all these decades, the ghost of Jack Shepard knew the layout at 122 Cranberry like the back of his hand — that is, like he used to know the back of his hand.

Six rooms occupied the second floor: a sunny eat-in kitchen with faded gold wall-paper and yellow curtains, a cozy living room with a smoke-stained fireplace and tall front windows, two large bedrooms, one child-size bedroom, and one bath. The old rooms were always kept tidy, but they showed the wear and age of an owner who had neither the wealth nor the youth to upgrade them.

The ghost of Jack Shepard tailed Penelope Thornton-McClure up the stairs and into those well-worn rooms. First stop: her son's bedroom, a ten-by-ten space in need of re-painting. The kid was still asleep on a small twin bed. Like the chest of drawers and nightstand, the white wood headboard displayed scratches and knicks, but the Curious George covers appeared clean and new. When Penelope kissed her son's copper bangs, he stirred.

"Mom?"

"Morning, honey. How did you sleep?"

The boy sat up. Yawned. Frowned. "Bad dream," he said.

"Again?" asked Penelope, sitting on the narrow bed. "Same kind?"

The kid nodded his head in the affirmative. Penelope hugged her son close and rocked him for a long minute.

Jack had been in Penelope's head for a while now, so he knew all about the kid — and her unending worry.

Apparently the kid had gone through grief counseling at school just after his father killed himself. At first, Penelope's instinct was to keep him close to her, but her in-laws pushed hard for her to "get him back to a normal routine." So, just as school ended, Spencer was sent away on his usual two weeks of foreign-language camp. After only one night, the kid called home, terrorized by nightmares, begging his mother to come get him.

"There's this rare genetic disease that I once read about in a novel, *familial dysautonomia,*" she'd told her Aunt Sadie early one morning over coffee. "One in something like four hundred thousand children are born with it — they cannot feel physical pain. This condition is quite dangerous because pain, when you think about, is actually useful, a valuable warning against hazards, illness, coming disease. No mother would want her child to suffer from *not* knowing he'd broken a bone or burned his finger. But when you see your child's face, completely bewildered, at his father's funeral; when you hear him crying at night that Daddy left, that he killed himself, and maybe you will, too — well, you can understand why I wished some rare genetic disease existed that prevented all forms of *emotional* pain."

Jack watched Penelope's fingers lightly stroke her son's hair. "I'm not going anywhere, honey. I'm right here. With you," she whispered. "And that's where I'm going to stay. We're in this together. You and me — and Aunt Sadie, too. And we're going to make this new life work. You got that?"

The boy's head, tucked tight to his mother's shoulder, nodded.

Mee-uuuwww . . .

At the bottom of the kid's bed, that little orange striped kitten they'd named "Bookmark" stirred and stretched and reached out its little orange paws. Jack didn't much go in for cute. But he supposed the furry thing was

97

okay. And it seemed to cheer up the kid, who reached out to pet the kitten's head.

The kitten began to purr. Then it stopped, arched its back, hissed at the corner where Jack was hanging, and fled from the room.

Damn stool-pigeon cat.

Pen stared after the kitten in obvious puzzlement. "She's probably hungry, don't you think?"

The boy nodded quickly.

"And I bet you are, too, right?"

"I suppose."

"Well, there's shredded wheat and blueberries on the table and milk in the fridge," said Penelope. "Pour some Kitten Chow for Bookmark, okay? I'll be in to eat with you in a few minutes. And after you eat breakfast and wash up, I'd like you to get dressed and come down and hang out with me and Aunt Sadie in the bookstore today, okay? Take a break from the TV for a little while."

"Aw, Mom, do I *have* to?" he said with another yawn.

"What do you think?" called Penelope as she left the room. The bath appeared to be the widow's next stop, which didn't discourage Jack's surveillance in the least.

Ancient aquamarine tiles covered the walls and floors; several were cracked, but all were spotlessly clean. Homemade shelves of rough blond wood held thick towels. A chipped old sink stood on a pedestal beside a small toilet.

And against the far wall sat a big claw-footed tub, around which hung a shower curtain with a marine life themed design.

Penelope kicked off her slingback shoes as soon as she stepped onto the tiled floor. He watched her reach behind the whales, dolphins, and their ilk to fiddle with the old porcelain handles. For a long minute, she stood there, letting the stream sluice between her fingers. "Too cold," she thought with calm annoyance. And then, "Too hot."

As she continued to let the water flow, Jack could hear its deep drumming as it beat against the tub. He could feel the steam building up in the bathroom air, see the fog forming on the mirror above the old chipped sink.

The small window of blue-and-green stained glass was wide open, and the warm September breeze blew in, its fragrance sweetened by roses on the town green. Pines from a nearby thicket offered a pungent streak, along with the slight tinge of marshy salt carried in from the ocean miles away.

The ghost of Jack Shepard recognized each of these scents. They were as distinct to him as the red, green, and yellow of the corner stoplight. Jack's body may have been dead for more than fifty years, but his state of awareness was very much alive.

Smells were stronger. Sounds were louder. Touch and taste were even possible in strange ways. And without any physical barriers to block his movements, he could now pass through furniture and floors, experiencing the feel of them on entirely new levels. Only the brick and mortar of this building were impenetrable to him, rendering him a prisoner here.

So what else was he going to do to pass the time? Surveillance work had been his profession — and, as they say, old habits die hard. Besides, the plain truth was, witnessing Timothy Brennan's murder had awakened Jack Shepard in peculiar new ways.

"A little too cold . . . almost there."

Jack heard Penelope's thoughts and wondered yet again what made this doll so special. He didn't know why, but he had to admit, he was curious.

First of all, in Jack's experience, communication with the living had been rare, limited mainly to giving all comers the shakes to the gate. The very idea that he could hear her thoughts at all was an oddity. Only two other beings in the last fifty-plus years had been able to broadcast their thoughts to him — and they had been children.

Second of all — and this was the real kicker — she could hear his passing thoughts whenever he desired it, and with the least amount of effort on his part. Never happened before, not to Jack. And with her prissy attitude irritating the hell out of him, Jack wasn't so sure he was very happy about it.

Case in point: Downstairs.

First, she refused to take his advice and give that insulting pink-cloaked goon of a councilwoman what for. Instead, she played the do-right girl, held her tongue to keep everything nicey-nice.

That sort of I'll-do-anything-to-keep-from-upsetting-the-applecart philosophy of living really grated on Jack. While a poker face was routinely necessary for the detection racket, when it came to family and friends, Jack believed that cards on the table, face up, was the only way to play it.

Next, she completely brushed off his warning that the State Police were here to find a perp to fit their profile. The once-over that detective-lieutenant gave Penelope had "you're a suspect" written all over it. Maybe that councilwoman tipped him, maybe he simply reviewed the witness statements from the night before, but he was making her for some sort of guilty party, and she refused to acknowledge it — yet another thing that grated on Jack: denial. Put your head in the sand and it'll all go away. That's *not* how Jack played the game, and if Penelope kept playing it her way, she'd be picked off like a clay pigeon at a sharpshooters' picnic.

"Ah, yes . . . that's the way I like it: warm . . . soothing . . . inviting."

Penelope had finally adjusted the water

temperature to her liking. Flipping up a central lever, she directed the flow through the shower nozzle above. Water rained down, and she leaned back to avoid its splash.

Stepping away from the curtain, she unzipped her wrinkled black skirt and let it pool at her feet on the tile floor. After stepping free of it, she slipped her fingers beneath the waistband of the pantyhose, whipping them off in one swift movement — much faster than Jack would have liked.

With an ethereal sigh, he remembered the old-style stockings that dames used to wear — garter belts holding up each silky leg separately. Some even put on a little grind for him, taking their good old time unsnapping them, rolling them off, their eyes watching his for a pleasurable reaction. A few dolls actually preferred to leave the silky stockings in place, removing only their panties so he could —

"You're not here, are you?"

Standing with hands on hips in her pale blue sweater set and virginal white panties, Penelope had addressed the empty air. Or at least it would have looked like empty air to the *living* eye.

He considered for a moment revealing himself to her. But he instantly thought better of it. He was simply having too much fun. For a dead guy, fun wasn't exactly a part of the daily vocab.

"You *better* not be here. I mean it."

Jack was dying to ask how she thought a "delusion" could spy on her in the shower, anyway. But he exercised self-control and kept silent.

Next she removed her glasses, then the loose blue sweater set, first shrugging off the exterior cardigan and then tugging the pull-over up and off.

An innocent cotton bra displayed ample mounds of flesh. Hers were the sort of generous curves Jack had favored when he'd been alive. And the sight of her womanly form, standing there in her bra and panties, struck Jack like a wall of bricks.

She seemed so vulnerable and soft, like the sweet idea of home. Here was everything he'd wanted in a woman . . . when he'd wanted a woman.

A longing washed over Jack, moving him. And, despite himself, he ached for something he knew he could never have.

Suddenly, he couldn't watch anymore. He retreated instead, back through the closed door, down the hallway, and into the living room. The digital television was on again and — once he adjusted the channel changer to a good crime show — it was sure to provide a much-needed distraction.

Chapter 9

Dying for Profit

You are not booksellers, you are re-
tailers. . . . You'll only win this battle if
you are damn good at something and provide the consumer with a better experience. . . . If you don't like change, you're
going to like irrelevance even less. . . .
The glory days for independent booksellers are gone.
— Tom Peters, keynote address, British
Booksellers Association, 2003

PROVIDENCE, RI (AP) — Last night's
death of internationally best-selling author
Timothy Brennan has cast an unusual
spotlight on Quindicott, Rhode Island, a
small hamlet just outside of Newport.

The site of Brennan's death was the
town's only bookstore. According to local
officials, he collapsed during a public talk
in which he announced *Shield of Justice*
would be his last Jack Shield novel.

An autopsy is being conducted by the
state medical examiner. In the meantime,
bids on eBay for first edition copies of

Shield of Justice bought at Buy the Book are topping $100.00 a copy.

Although sales of Jack Shield novels had floundered in the midnineties, Brennan's most recent efforts were the strongest he'd ever written, according to critics, and an upcoming feature film deal was reportedly in the making. Consequently, Brennan's abrupt announcement that he intended to stop writing Shield novels shocked his fans and the publishing world.

"Quitting while you're ahead isn't an unheard-of strategy," said Parker Peterson, president and publisher of Salient House, "but Tim had just hit his stride again. So, of course, it was a shock to us."

Brennan's death was also a shock to his fans and even his third and most recent wife, who had chosen to remain in the couple's New York City apartment rather than accompany her husband on his book tour.

"He had a weak heart, sure," said Mrs. "Bunny" Brennan, "but it wasn't *that* bad, you know? Timmy *just* had a physical. He wanted to make sure he was healthy enough to make the book tour, you know? — and he was, too. The doctor said he was fit as a fiddle. I'm really, really shocked."

The store, which now goes by the name Buy the Book, was the last place detective

Jack Shepard had been seen before his disappearance nearly fifty years before, Brennan said. Shepard was the real-life model for Brennan's Jack Shield character, star of nineteen novels and two TV series.

Brennan also revealed he planned to write his next and last book as a nonfiction investigation into Jack Shepard's last unsolved case.

"Pen! Can . . . you . . . believe . . . this?!"

I was standing behind the counter next to Sadie, helping her ring up and bag. The Staties had let us reopen at one o'clock, and three hours later, Linda Cooper-Logan was jumping up and down in front of me, trying to lift her head of short, spiky blond hair above the crush of customers crowding the Buy the Book checkout area.

"Linda, what are you doing here?" I called. "Doesn't Milner need you at the bakery?"

"Closed — an hour ago!"

"Why?"

"Sold . . . everything!"

"For heaven's sake, Linda, come around the counter." I lifted the hinged section of heavy oak and shouted into the crowd: "Let this woman through, please!"

Outside, the cobblestone streets of Quindicott were jammed with cars, and Buy the Book's aisles were packed with customers. I still would have been guessing the reason why if Seymour Tarnish, our mailman (and the biggest local celebrity since his recent win on *Jeopardy!*), hadn't stopped by to inform us that a tiny Associated Press sidebar about Buy the Book — which included news of inflated bidding on eBay for copies of *Shield of Justice* purchased at our store — was being featured beside Brennan's *New York Times* obituary on one of the most visited of World Wide Web addresses, the Drudge Report.

According to Seymour, local radio stations had started discussing the death of Brennan, the bidding for the books — and our store. This explained the crowds descending, along with local television camera crews looking to interview me and Sadie.

"I brought you all the last of Milner's five-nut tarts," said Linda, holding the pastry box high as she swam through the jostling bodies and lunged behind the counter. "I thought you might be hungry over here."

"Excuse me!" a loud voice called. "Do you have any more copies of *Shield of Justice*? The display is empty."

"Empty!" cried a chorus of horrified voices as a new crowd pushed through the front door.

"Keep your pants on, people!" called Sadie. "We have plenty of copies —"

"I have some! I have some!" Spencer called, hurrying toward the front of the store, his arms filled with jacketed hardcovers.

For hours, my son had been helping us behind the counter. Just ten minutes ago he'd taken his first break — to visit the rest room. Obviously, he'd decided to make a side trip to the stockroom. He set down the stack of books and began placing them into the empty display like a seasoned floor manager.

Someone reached over his head to snag a copy.

"Guess they don't have child labor laws in Rhode Island," a middle-aged man near the register quipped to his companion.

Lawyer joke. Ha-ha.

"Whoever is driving a black BMW convertible with Connecticut plates, please move it. You're blocking my SUV!" shouted a woman through the front door.

Spencer appeared at my side, his face flushed. "The display was filled," he said excitedly, "but it's going to be empty real soon. I'll have to bring out more books."

I handed him a tart from the Cooper Family Bakery box. "Honey, go upstairs, pour a glass of milk, and take a break, okay?"

"I'll get some milk, but then I'm coming right back down!" he replied. "You need me. I'm your official stamper, you know!"

"I know, honey, but I don't want you to get too tired," I said, remembering how sensitive his father had been to any form of exertion.

Calvin never could endure any sort of tension for long. He said hard work was too upsetting for him. Stomach-churning. No way to live. Of course, Calvin had ultimately decided *living* itself was no way to live, either.

"I'll be right back. I'm not tired at all." Then, nut tart raised high, he parted the crowd, announcing, "Don't worry, folks. We have plenty of copies of that *Shield* book!"

The transformation from indifferent kid to dedicated bookseller seemed nothing short of miraculous to me.

"He looks happy for once," said Linda.

"It's simple," said Sadie. "Being needed is the best medicine, and right now we need all the help we can get."

"Ab-sh-o-lulley!" I garbled around the nut tart, stuffed into my cheeks like a famished squirrel.

"Milner says if we have a few more days like this, we can finally afford that new awning," said Linda as Sadie and I continued to ring up and bag the customers' purchases.

"It's entirely possible," I said. "Sadie and I gave three television interviews so far today."

"Ohmygod, we're rich," said Linda. "Your store's put Quindicott on the map!"

"Well, tell that to our favorite councilwoman," I said.

"The Municipal Zoning Witch? Why?" asked Linda.

"She stopped by this morning, primarily to

threaten us," I said.

"Oh, yeah," said Sadie. "Pinkie was in rare form. She predicted our author appearance fiasco last night would turn the town's economic clock backward."

"Well, I never knew this town *had* an economic clock," said Linda. "But if it does, I'd say you two set it to running on fast forward. Franzetti's Pizza and Sam's Seafood Shack is jammed. The gas station has a line around the block, Colleen's turning away manicure customers, and Seymour's ice cream truck looks like a mosh pit."

"A mosh what?" asked Sadie.

"It's kind of like when bobby-soxers used to rush the stage at a Sinatra concert," Linda explained.

"Geez, Louise, you don't have to go back that far," said Sadie. "An *Elvis* analogy would have sufficed."

"Speaking of mosh pits," I said, "we're going to be in the middle of one ourselves if we don't get more books on the floor."

"I'll go," said Sadie. "Linda, you take over Spencer's place? Pen can ring up the purchases."

"Hey, whoever works here!" called a male voice near the floor display. "Your Brennan display is almost empty again!"

Sadie flipped up the hinged counter. "Well, as that Statie detective put it this morning, looks like death is good for business."

"Okay," said Linda, "put me to work. What was Spence doing, anyway?"

"Stamping and bagging," I said.

"Bagging I've heard of, but what the heck is 'stamping'?"

"It's simple," I said, slapping the rubber stamper into her hand. As I spoke, I rang up another sale: four copies of *Shield of Justice*, the latest Janet Evanovich, and a book from our out-of-print section, one of the first U.S. editions of Agatha Christie's *Murder on the Orient Express* — published by Dodd, Mead in 1934 as *Murder in the Calais Coach*. (I was gratified to see customers buying other titles in addition to Brennan's book.)

I handed the purchases to Linda, opening the *Shield of Justice* cover, and pointed.

"Oh, I see!" said Linda as she pressed the stamper down. The ink branded the inside front cover with a simple seal: an open book surrounded by a magnifying glass and the words PROPERTY OF BUY THE BOOK. "Oooo! Nice touch," she said.

"Spence was the one who thought of it," I said, ringing up the next customer. "When we first opened today, this nice, soft-spoken gentleman asked for a book plate from the store — he wanted some way to mark the book as having been purchased here. And Spence remembered how we rubber-stamp our incoming cartons — so he stamped the man's book personally.

"You know, the man even called him 'Spenser for Hire,' and now Spence thinks he's named after a Robert B. Parker private detective. It made him happy, so I didn't remind him that he's actually named after a McClure."

"Pen!" called Sadie not ten minutes later. "There's some people to see you."

I looked up to find two familiar faces approaching the counter.

"Good afternoon, Mrs. McClure," said Timothy Brennan's daughter, Deirdre Brennan-Franken.

She doesn't look good. That was my first impression, and it had nothing to do with fashion. In fact, her emerald suit with matching scarf was as impeccably tailored as the burgundy outfit she'd worn the night before. But today her cheeks were sunken, her red hair unwashed, her eyes bloodshot. She looked as though she'd been crying all night.

Beside her, Kenneth Franken stood, wearing that same beautiful camel-hair jacket, a fresh white shirt, open-collared, and pressed brown slacks.

"I'm sorry to bother you," said Deirdre, "with your store so busy and everything, but . . ."

I immediately lifted up the counter, and Sadie took my place at the register. Then I ushered Deirdre and Kenneth away from the crowded main store and into the quieter

112

community events space. After I set up a few folding chairs, we all sat.

"I wanted to come by sooner," said Deirdre, "but we had a lot to take care of, speaking to family members, my father's lawyer, and the state investigators had so many questions." She glanced at her husband, who looked especially uncomfortable with the mention of the police.

"I'm so sorry about what happened, Mrs. Franken. The way he died, right in front of you. It's quite a shock, something like that, I know from personal experience. You should really be taking it easy — give yourself time to grieve. . . ."

Suddenly Deirdre burst into tears, putting her head in her hands. I looked at Kenneth, who frowned and quickly pulled out a hand-kerchief for her. He didn't need it, I noted; his eyes were as dry as petrified bone.

"That's the trouble, Mrs. McClure," she said as she wiped her eyes. "A part of me is actually *glad* he's dead."

"You shouldn't say that," I told her. And yet a secret part of me understood com-pletely. Not so much because of Timothy Brennan, but Calvin McClure.

"I know, I know," said Deirdre. "It's ter-rible. But it's how I feel. He was a contempt-ible man. Thoroughly selfish and so very cruel — a bully really, especially to Ken —"

"You still shouldn't say it," I warned. "I

113

mean, I know it's how you feel, and I know that's the truth of death — that it can stir up many things, as much resentment and rage as anything else, but the reason you shouldn't say it is because the State Police are investigating his death. And you don't want to give them the wrong idea. Especially if you're inheriting anything."

"I'm inheriting everything," said Deirdre. "It *all* comes to me. Even his third wife isn't getting a penny — because he'd already grown tired of her and was planning a divorce."

"Then you really should keep your feelings private," I said.

"Oh, that's what Ken told me, too, but the cat's out of the bag. I blurted out exactly how I felt to that State Police lieutenant this morning. Marsh's investigation is a waste of time, anyway." She waved her hand as if it were behind her already. "The autopsy results will clear all that up. My father had a weak heart. It's obvious that's why he died."

"Well, I really wouldn't give any more statements," I said. "Your lawyer should be the one to do that."

"That's what I told her," said Ken Franken.

"That's right, but I'm quite able to speak for myself. That's partly why I came back to see you. I wanted to have a press conference here when the autopsy results come in," said

Deirdre. "Would that be all right?"

"Of course," I said.

"And . . . this is really trivial, but earlier today I couldn't find my makeup bag, and I can only think that I must have left it in the ladies' room here last night. I'm so scatterbrained sometimes before my father speaks that I tend to do that sort of thing. Anyway, I did check back there, but it's gone. Your aunt intercepted me. She said she didn't know anything about it, but she suggested I speak to you. Did you find it? It's a small red zipper bag, monogrammed with my initials."

I shifted uneasily. "Mrs. Franken, if you left your makeup bag in our rest room, I'm afraid the State Police forensic team has it now."

"What?" Kenneth Franken rose in outrage, his tall frame towering over both Deirdre and me.

"I'm sorry," I said, "but they were here this morning, bagging and tagging the leftover food and drinks and anything else suspicious they could find."

"How could you let them?!" cried Ken.

I stood up. "I'm sorry, Mr. Franken, but they didn't *ask*. They had a warrant."

"Ken, please," said Deirdre, jumping between us. "Don't take it out on poor Mrs. McClure."

"I'm going to look myself," said Ken, fuming.

"Dear, it's the *ladies'* room," said Deirdre.

"So I'll knock first," he said. "Excuse me."

Kenneth strode away, none too happy, and Deirdre turned to me. "I'm so sorry about that, Mrs. McClure. Ken and I . . . we've had our marital troubles, you know? And I think Ken has been overprotective of me in hopes of showing me . . . showing me he wants to make things up. I hope you understand."

"Of course," I said. "Please don't worry about anything. I'm sure it will all work out just fine. And in the meantime, why don't you stop by Colleen's Beauty Shop? She has a line of cosmetics that I'm sure will hold you over until you can get your own things back."

"It's a shame," said Deirdre.

"About your father?"

"About my makeup bag. I had some imported skin treatments in there. Quite expensive." Deirdre sighed and shook her head. "Oh, well." Then she looked up and around the room — the same room where her father had expired less than twenty-four hours before.

Finally her eyes met mine. "I cried all night, Mrs. McClure. So don't think I'm not sorry to lose him. He may have been a bastard . . . but he was my father."

"I understand. More than you know, Mrs.

Franken. And if there's anything more I can do . . ."

She shook her head, and when Kenneth Franken returned, they departed, empty-handed.

Chapter 10

Inquiring Minds

"You goofed, Fletcher. You goofed big."
"What did I do?"
"You quoted somebody who's been dead
for two years . . ."
"Who says he's dead?"
— Managing Editor Frank Jaffee, trying
to fire reporter Irwin Fletcher in *Fletch
and the Widow Bradley* by Gregory Mc-
donald, 1981

By sunset, the crowd had thinned and the
streets of Old Q were quieting down. There
were about twenty people left browsing —
more than Sadie used to get in an entire
week before we'd renovated — but by today's
yardstick, the store was practically deserted.

After we polished off a Franzetti's cheese
pizza on our feet, I sent Spence upstairs with
a *children's* mystery under his arm, thank
goodness. He'd wanted to read a "Spenser
for Hire" story, but I showed him that Mr.
Parker's books were a little too long and too
complicated for a boy his age to read (not to
mention too violent and risqué).

I slyly suggested he start his mystery reading with a book that would help him improve his reading ability, so he could one day read all about his namesake: Spenser for Hire. That did the trick. He picked out Louis Sachar's Newbery-winning *Holes*, and announced he was going to read every book in the children's section by next summer. Then he was off.

"Someone's checking you out," Linda whispered to me as she helped me ring up one of the last few customers.

"Who?" I asked. "The guy over there?" I cocked my head in the general direction of a balding man in his forties wearing khakis and a green sweater. He was lurking in the used-book section, a Buy the Book bag tucked under his arm.

"That's a collector," Sadie interjected. "Along with the Brennan book he bought a copy of Colin Wilson's *Ritual in the Dark* from the resale section. Recognized a bargain when he saw one — an out-of-print first edition with dust jacket, in not too shabby condition."

Linda blinked as if Sadie were speaking in tongues. "*Ritual in the Dark*? Never heard of that one," she said.

"It's a British thriller set in the 1960s, but based on the murders of Jack the Ripper," said Sadie. "And considering his taste in reading, I'd say date the guy with caution."

"Thank goodness I wasn't talking about *him* then," Linda said. "I meant *that* one!"

Linda nodded in a direction vaguely to the left of the green-sweater guy. I shifted my gaze and ran smack into the eyes of a handsomeish man in his midthirties with large, perfect teeth; slicked-back, dark brown hair; and round Harry Potter-esque glasses.

I don't know why, but the idea that he might be a car salesman came to mind. That or an actor. Must have been the teeth.

To my surprise, the man's smile grew when our eyes met. Suddenly he was crossing the store, making a beeline toward me.

"What do you think he wants?" I whispered, acutely aware I was still rather hung over. Last time I'd glanced in the restroom mirror, I'd had red eyes, drawn skin, and smeared lipstick.

"He's sort of cute," Linda said in the perky *go-get-him* tone I hadn't heard her use on me since junior high. "Nice threads, too."

Before I could answer Linda, the man's creased khakis, snow-white button-down, and tailored navy jacket were heading right for me. The toothy smile came at me with such dazzling brilliance I briefly considered installing him permanently in our dimly lit back room.

"Hi, there. I'm a senior editor with *Independent Bookseller* magazine. I was in the area, and I thought I might take a few notes for a story about your charming store."

I stepped around the counter and stood toe to toe with the man. He was only about two inches taller than I, which wasn't very tall for a man since I'm a shoeless five-four, but he was more than passing fit. The jacket did little to disguise the fact that he was plenty musclebound, with very broad shoulders and a thick neck and arms.

"Howie Westwood," he said brightly, holding out his hand.

Wow, I thought. The guy's energy level almost spiked my own wattage shortage. "Hello," I managed as I reached to shake. "I'm Penelope Thornton-McClure."

He took my hand in his and looked into my eyes. "Pleased to meet you, Penelope. Oh, excuse me. *May* I call you Penelope?"

"Yes, of course." He was still holding my hand. I eased my grip, but he held on. The guy was strong. Somewhere amid my responding hormones, I registered the fact that his palms felt callused. A yachtsman? I wondered.

"You must be the owner —" he began.

"Co-owner," I cut in, correcting him. "My aunt is the original owner. Sadie Thornton." I gestured toward her with my free hand and he lifted his chin at her — a little too dismissively, I thought. And didn't appreciate. I tugged my hand back.

"This is truly a unique space," Howie said

121

with easy admiration. "Quite an achievement. You must have considerable retail experience."

"Thank you," I said. And that's all I said. The guy was attractive; Linda was right about that. But that was no reason to instantly trust him.

"You wouldn't think a town as small as Quindicott could support a store of this size."

A fair question, and an observant one, I decided. Okay, maybe the guy was good at what he did. "Well, plenty of tourists pass through here on their way to Newport and the Cape," I said. "You'd be surprised at how many. And we have a considerable mail order business. Out-of-print books, rare first printings, special editions."

"Web site?"

"Not yet, but it's on the drawing boards," I lied. I'd been way too busy to figure that one out — but maybe by the time the article ran, I'd get something under e-construction.

I felt Sadie's eyes on my back and stole a glance in her direction. She was smiling and nodding — the matchmaker nod. *Eeeesh.* I shot back the warning look: I am *not* in the market for a match, thank you very much!

"Of course, like everyone else, I heard about the incident last night, and about Timothy Brennan's death," Howie Westwood said.

"Yes," I said, frowning. "A terrible thing."

"Not really so terrible for you, though, right? I mean, business looks pretty good. You and your aunt seem to be profiting nicely from Brennan's death."

For a moment, I was speechless. It was true. He was right. I couldn't deny it. But hearing it stated so coldly, so matter-of-factly . . . it made me feel awful.

"We didn't plan for this to happen," I finally murmured. "And as you can see, we haven't raised the price of the book, despite the inflated bidding on eBay. We're not trying to take advantage — we're just handling the customers who've come to us. And I assure you, Mr. Westwood, Brennan's death was a terrible thing to witness."

"Witness . . . yes," Howie continued. "And the whole thing unfolding in front of his daughter and son-in-law. They were right here attending the talk, right? Were they close to Mr. Brennan when he . . . was stricken?"

I wasn't surprised by his questions. But with autopsy results still pending and Brennan's family still in Quindicott, I felt it was the proper thing to duck any touchy questions — just as I'd ducked them with the television interviews earlier in the day.

Television . . . my mind considered the fact that a few of those interviews had already aired. I suddenly wondered if that was why

Howie was here. Had he seen one of those interviews and — noting the lack of details — decided to come by himself and try his hand at prying them loose? Well, I couldn't blame the guy for trying, I decided. But still, I held firm:

"Many people attended last night's event," I told him. "And many people rushed to Mr. Brennan's aid. I think it's best if you ask Mr. Brennan's family these questions. They're staying right here in town, at Finch's Inn. It's on the eastern edge of town, on the pond. Well, we call it a pond, but it's really a small lake at the end of a coastal inlet."

"Of course," Howie Westwood replied. Though the smile was still plastered on his face, behind his little round glasses I saw a cold curtain draw down across the man's green eyes.

"Could you show me around?" he said, his charm returning, a little more forced this time.

"Sure," I said.

After all, like *Publishers Weekly*, *Independent Bookseller* was a respected magazine in the industry of bookselling, especially for its often-quoted review section. Its circulation had fallen off in the past decade, of course, with the closing of so many independent bookstores — due to the gross sales dollars of the book business being hijacked by the chain stores (and I'm not just talking Borders and

Barnes & Noble, but also places such as Costco, Wal-Mart, and Sam's Club, where you could toss your Grisham in a cart with your economy crates of grapefruit and galoshes).

In any event, I wanted to be cooperative. An article in *Independent Bookseller* would be lovely for Buy the Book. It would influence publicists to put our store on their "A list" author tours, and it might even get Sadie and me invited to some of those boffo celebrity book parties thrown by big publishers at next May's BEA (BookExpo America, that is, the nation's largest trade show for publishers and booksellers).

I showed Howie the store, talked about the strategy for moving inventory, the customer base, the Shaker rockers, the renovations — everything and anything except the traumatic events of the night before. He took notes by way of a small tape recorder.

Each time he broached the subject of my opinion of Timothy Brennan and his family and the play-by-play of his death the night before — and there were more than a few times when he did — I answered by being as politely vague as possible (I lived with my prying in-laws long enough to become familiar with that sort of lingual dexterity).

Finally we reached the community events space, right near the podium Timothy Brennan was standing behind when he collapsed. Howie Westwood again pressed me for details about the incident. He couldn't miss the tone of impatience I now had in my voice as I replied,

"Look, why don't you interview Shelby Cabot? She was the woman in charge of the publicity tour for Salient House and —"

"Penelope, *come on*. She's Salient House's spokesperson." He stared at me.

"Yes. Meaning?"

"Meaning her mouth is programmed to speak only in empty corporate syllables. She's never going to give me any real details — the sort of details that will make the article on your bookstore worth reading, if you catch my meaning."

"Oh, I catch your meaning." I folded my arms. "Sorry, Charlie."

"The name's Howie."

"Yes. I know."

He blinked, his smile disappearing. Then, smoothly, it reappeared. "You're sure a tough one, Penelope, I'll give you that. Okay, then, I'll look her up."

His charm was still there, but his polish was dimming, and I began to wonder if he wasn't some other kind of reporter — like maybe from a supermarket tabloid. I nearly shuddered as a headline flashed through my mind: CURSED BOOKSTORE PROVOKES FAMOUS AUTHOR'S DEATH. ARE MORE IN STORE?

"I had better get back to the register," I said after an awkward pause.

"Of course," Howie said, nodding. "I'll just take a few notes about the look of the room if that's okay."

"Yes, of course," I said. Then I raced to the front counter.

"Whoa, honey, where's the fire?" said Aunt Sadie.

"What happened?" asked Linda. "Did he ask you out to dinner? Do you want to check your makeup?"

"No, no, no, for heaven's sake!" I cried, bending under the counter to search the shelves. "Where is it?! Where is it?!"

"Where's what?" the two women chorused.

"HERE!"

I snatched up my latest copy of *Independent Bookseller*, which I always kept alphabetically above issues of *Kirkus*, *Library Journal*, select printouts of an inner-circle e-newsletter called *Publishers Lunch*, and *Publishers Weekly*.

"Where'd you leave lover boy?" asked Sadie.

"In the events room," I said. "And don't call him that!"

"What are you looking for?" asked Linda as I flipped the front pages of the magazine until I reached the masthead.

My finger followed the small print down to the names of the staff writers. "Ohmygod, it really is him."

"Him who?" asked Linda. "Lover boy?"

I shot her an unhappy look and pointed to the magazine page. Sure enough, the name was there: Howie Westwood, Senior Editor.

"What's the matter?" asked Sadie.

"I thought he was lying — that he was from a supermarket tabloid or something."

"Did you blow it?" asked Linda.

"I think so," I said. I hadn't played ball. I'd been mildly hostile. And he'd implied some pretty caustic things about the store's connection to the Brennan death. That was sure to reflect itself in the tone he used to write about the store.

"It's not too late," said Linda. "Invite him out tonight."

"No!"

"Don't be foolish," said Sadie. "You deserve some fun. And the man obviously likes you."

"You think?" I said. A pathetic equivocation.

"For sure," said Linda. "And he's a cutey. Go get him."

"It's really not like that," I insisted. "It's just business."

Right, I thought. Who are you kidding? Certainly not them.

I put down the magazine and headed down the aisle. Along the way, I ran a hand through my copper tangles, adjusted my black-framed glasses, and straightened my loose white blouse.

128

Okay, there were things about Westwood that seemed a little too slick, a little too smooth, but it had been a long time since my late husband and I had . . . well, *connected* . . . on any level. At least Westwood reported on the book business, so we had something to talk about. And Sadie and Linda seemed to think he liked me. Maybe offering to show him around town wouldn't be too forward.

I was barely able to catch him at the front door. "Mr. Westwood?"

"Oh, uh, Mrs. McClure. Thank you for your time."

"No problem. I just wanted to tell you that I really do think Shelby Cabot will be helpful for your story," I said, trying to make up for my earlier frostiness. "She's staying at Finch's Inn, too, with the Brennan family, and she can probably even get you the names of those two young cameramen."

"Cameramen?" Howie Westwood's eyes widened behind his little round glasses.

"Yes," I said. "Two young men taped the whole event for C-SPAN. Didn't you know that?"

Howie Westwood paled. "*Nobody* knows that. At least, I haven't seen it reported."

"Anyway, before you go, I was wondering . . ."

"Yes?"

Ask him, ask him, ask him! I railed at myself. *Come on, Pen, don't be such a wuss.*

"Would you like me to show you around town?" I asked, my voice betraying me with a slight flirtatious lilt. "I mean, I thought the background could help your article about our store . . . maybe we could even get a cup of coffee or dinner. . . ."

The transparent reaction flashed across his features in a matter of seconds. It started out as a sour sort of squint of discomfort, then it softened into a kind of pained pity, then it hardened again, into a mask with a shallow, toothy grin and a chilly green stare.

I wanted to crawl into a hole right then and there.

He didn't come right out and say, "You've got to be kidding. Me and *you?*" It was more like, "Oh, sure . . . *maybe* in a few days I *might* take you up on that," and then he lunged for the door.

Yes, a deep, dark hole. That's what I needed right now. Put me in. Cover me up.

The only thing that *might* keep me out was turning around to find Sadie and Linda *not* eavesdropping.

Slowly, I turned. Then exhaled with relief. They were both chatting and laughing with an elderly male customer, completely oblivious to my naked embarrassment.

"Thank goodness," I murmured.

About the only thing worse than being utterly and completely rejected was having someone else witness it.

Screw the ass.

"Oh, no. Not you."

Yes, me. The Jack Shepard voice was deep and rough and loud in my head.

"You're not real," I silently told it. "And I'm not listening."

Forget that moron. He's not who he's pretending to be. I'd make book on it.

"Get lost. I mean it!"

I was in no mood to talk to Jack's voice, but he was loud and insistent — and, even though I knew he wasn't real, his invasion of my privacy felt real enough. Frankly, I was indignant.

I don't know, doll. Seems to me you need a private eye on your side around here — even one who got lead poisoning fifty years back.

"And what makes you think so?"

Howie Westwood.

"What about him?"

He conned you.

"How do you know that?"

Simple observations, sugar. That's all it took. The guy's as phony as a three-dollar bill.

"Shows what you know. Or what you don't. He's a magazine writer. His name's listed in the *Independent Bookseller* staff box."

So the hood found a good cover? So what? That doesn't explain the contradictions.

"What contradictions?"

You ought to try picking up a few pointers

131

from some of the books you sell around here. Look, I know you noticed the guy was muscle-bound. His grip alone practically made you wince. You noticed the calluses, too. How many bookworms you know look like they can punch out a street cop?

"He could have been a *fit* bookworm," Penelope said. "He did have glasses, which is common among people who make their living reading."

Fake.

"Fake?"

The glass was clear. Not prescription. I'll give you a pass on noticing that one, since you couldn't get close enough. But I could. And did.

"But . . ."

Yeah?

"Those little round frames give a man a certain look," I silently said. "He might be wearing them as a fashion statement."

Doll, repeat after me: Men. Do not. Make fashion statements.

"Maybe they didn't in your time. But they do now. Oh, why am I speaking to you as if you're really the ghost of Jack Shepard?!! You're just a voice. A stupid, silly voice in my head."

And another thing — those set of pearly whites. Big, perfect ivories like that don't happen in nature. God can't even afford to give sets like that away. And, as far as I know, neither can a small magazine like the one your "Howie" claimed he worked for —

"He's not my Howie —"

So tell me, doll, how many people in the book publishing game can afford that set of choppers? Not many, I'd wager. But it's the sort of mouth job someone in a high-priced profession could afford. What does that tell you?

"Nothing. Just like you."

You're just stung 'cause nothing came of giving that chump the glad eye —

"Excuse me, but if you insist on speaking, would you mind speaking English?"

Don't get your panties in a bunch, sister. I'm speaking English, all right. You gave Howie Westwood the glad eye. You were looking him over good, flirting with him, even fantasizing a few racy things if I'm not mistaken.

"I most certainly was not!"

Spin your yarns for Auntie, not me.

"What?!"

You're not married anymore. So why be ashamed of admitting to a new attraction?

Penelope sighed. "I wasn't attracted. Not really. I just wondered —"

Yeah, I get it. You wanted to know if you could still get a Joe hot in the zipper. Well, you certainly could have in my time, doll. You're what we called whistle bait — and if I were alive, you and me, we'd be heating up your sheets in no time flat.

Penelope couldn't believe a mere delusion

was making her flush scarlet. "Must you be so vulgar?"

What is it about you fair-play Janes wanting prissy little packages? Everything's got to be presented all neat and pretty and correct. But guess what, doll, life ain't like that. People aren't like that. They're angry and jealous and ugly and weak — and full of primal feelings, as you well know.

"They're not all that way. People can be good. And fair. And courageous and selfless. My mother was. My father was . . . for a while, before my mother died. And my aunt definitely is — and so are the good people of this town."

Verdict's out on your townie friends, sweetheart. But I'll be watching.

"I wish you wouldn't," I said. Then I raised my chin, turned on my heel, and strode back toward the checkout counter. Thankfully, the Jack Shepard delusion of mine didn't follow.

Chapter 11

Shadow Boxing

Midnight, I dare say. . . . That's the word.
The time when the graves give up their
dead, and ghosts walk.
— Dashiell Hammett,
The Dain Curse, 1928

Two hours later, at three minutes after nine,
Sadie rang up the last of the day's *Shield of
Justice* purchases for a well-dressed, middle-
aged couple who also had a taste for the
Kellermans — Jonathan and Faye.

No longer capable of smiles, I wisely let
Sadie answer their chatty questions and politely send them on their way. The moment
they departed, I threw the lock, flipped the
sign to read CLOSED, and fell against the
door.

"Tired?" Aunt Sadie asked. As she began
to empty the register and count the day's receipts, I collapsed into a nearby chair and
stared vacantly at the intentionally rustic
charm of the exposed beams in our ceiling.

"Now, why would I be tired?" I replied.
"Could it be that I was living through one of

the most eventful days in my life with a horrendous hangover — the result of alcohol ingested at your urging, by the way? Or maybe it was the threat from Councilwoman Binder-Smith to shut us down? Or the State Police raid that pretty much capped our morning — and all this before we opened for business?"

Sadie clicked her tongue. "You're babbling, dear. And, anyway, we can't help it if a famous author drops dead in our store, now, can we?"

"What if Timothy Brennan didn't just drop dead?" I asked, finally coming out with the question that had been nagging at me all day. "What if the autopsy suggests foul play? Lieutenant Marsh will want to pin the crime on someone."

"What if pigs had wings?" said Aunt Sadie with a snort.

As I watched Sadie rubber-band thick wads of cash, my "babbling" continued. "If Brennan *was* the victim of foul play, then the suspect list would include those who had opportunity, access, and, of course, motive, which means we could be on the list."

"How do you figure that?"

"For better or worse, Brennan's death put Buy the Book on the map, didn't it? I mean, look at all that cash — in one day's take. We're making money because Brennan died here. And I really didn't want to admit this to you — or even to myself, frankly — but

Lieutenant Marsh looked me up and down this morning like I was guilty."

"Of what?"

"Anything. Anything he can make stick. I'm sure of it. And that's what worries me. You and I both know the state won't take over a local investigation unless they're asked — and Councilwoman Marjorie Binder-Smith almost certainly insisted, no doubt with a tip-off to watch *me* for suspicious behavior."

"Don't be silly," Aunt Sadie replied. "You're just overtired." But this time her dismissal lacked conviction. I could see my words had made her begin to worry, too.

Aunt Sadie stuffed the day's receipts into a threadbare canvas bag, which she'd used since she first took over the store from her father decades ago. She tied the bag with its frayed, gray string, tucked it under her arm and headed for the stairs.

"I'm going to bed, sweetie," Sadie called over her shoulder. "Don't forget to turn out the lights before you come upstairs. See you in the morning."

Despite my tired feet, I was wired. Worrying will do that to a person. I thought some surfing time on the Internet might help distract me, but first I had to close down the rest of the store.

I moved through the lighted aisles to a bank of electrical controls near the entrance to the community events space. Flicking switches, I shut down all but the recessed security lights in the ceiling.

The entire interior of Buy the Book was now dark, illuminated only by a dull glow that cast deep shadows between the tall bookshelves. Outside the high windows, the night-cloaked streets of Quindicott had gone quiet.

At the end of the block, the hanging stoplight at the crossroad swung in the nighttime breeze, blinking from green to yellow to red, signaling traffic that wasn't there.

Even the formerly cheerful community events space seemed slightly menacing, its cavernous interior, where a corpse had lain just twenty-four hours ago, blanketed in darkness.

With a sudden shiver, I turned, intending to head back to the main store's register area when I heard a strange, hollow, banging sound. The noise had come from somewhere inside the darkened community events room.

Trying not to panic, I listened intently. When the sound came again, louder this time, I forced the rational part of my mind to identify the odd yet strangely familiar noise.

"Jack?" I whispered to my delusion. "Is that you? If you're trying to scare me with some pretense of ghostly manifestation — well, it isn't very funny."

No reply. My Jack Shepard alter ego was missing in action.

Typical.

Where's a psychotic delusion of a ghostly detective when you really need one?

Despite my better judgment, I carefully tiptoed into the darkened community events room in an effort to discover the source of the banging sound.

I tried not to think about my eerie dream the night before, the ghostly presence, the upside-down chairs, the construction workers' weekly complaints of vanishing and reappearing tools.

Perhaps a squirrel — or even a raccoon — had somehow gotten in through the back door. It had happened before. After all, there were plenty of woods around the town, and the animals were known to root through garbage for food scraps.

That explanation sounded credible enough to make me bold, and within a few moments I had pretty much convinced myself that this was the case, which is why I kept the lights off. Turning them on again might scare the critter.

It was only after I had completely crossed the creepy emptiness of the community events room that I had second thoughts.

What if I were wrong, and it wasn't some cute, furry squirrel making all that racket? What if it was a raving mad, *rabid* raccoon — with sharp claws and ripping teeth! Or worse, what if the noise was caused by an intruder? A burglar, or worse? And here I was, confronting him alone, without even a weapon.

By this time I spied a sliver of light shining out from under a lavatory door, which didn't alarm me at first because the switches for those lights weren't controlled by the master.

Then I heard the sound again. Hearing it in context, this time, I knew what it was. In fact, I heard it twice a week when I removed the aluminum covers from the paper towel dispensers to refill them.

Before I could puzzle out why a squirrel would jump four feet in the air to mess with a paper towel dispenser, the door to the women's room burst open, blinding me with the explosive glare of fluorescent light.

I yelped, and someone grunted. The dark silhouette of a man appeared in the doorway. The figure lurched forward, and the door closed behind it. Once again the world was plunged into darkness — only now my night vision was a blurry mess of fluorescent afterglow.

A body crashed into me. Fingers gripped my shoulders and held on. With a scream, I tore free of the intruder's grasp and ran across the darkened room.

"Wait!" a voice cried.

But I wasn't stopping. Despite my impaired vision, I crossed the room in record time, arms outstretched like Frankenstein's monster. Finally I stumbled over my own feet and smacked into the wall. Reaching out, my fingers closed on the light switches and I flipped every last one.

The room brightened, and with my vision restored, I turned to face the intruder. "Don't you come near me or —"

Or *what* I didn't know. Fortunately, it didn't matter.

"Mrs. McClure! It's me. Josh! Josh Bernstein from Salient House. Shelby Cabot's assistant!"

"Josh?"

"I'm so embarrassed," Josh Bernstein said. "I came to the store a little before closing time, just to say hello and see how things were going. But suddenly I felt a little sick . . ."

He rubbed his stomach as if to emphasize the problem.

"I went to the rest room, and I guess I was there a long time. I didn't realize you had closed the store . . . I guess I'm lucky I wasn't locked in all night!"

Needless to say, I felt like an idiot. I apologized for reacting so hysterically, and politely offered to make him some tea. He refused, saying he just wanted to return to Finch's Inn and go to bed.

Privately relieved, I unlocked the door, and he departed.

My heart was still beating fast from the fright as Josh stopped to look at me through the window. When he saw me looking back, he offered a forced sort of half smile before vanishing into the night.

The Salient House publicity assistant seemed just as shaken up as I, and I wanted to dismiss it on face value.

But I couldn't. "Because his story didn't explain why he'd come out of the *women's* room," I murmured.

You said it, doll!

My Jack delusion was back. And I was pissed. "Where have you been?" I demanded. "I could have used some company a few minutes ago."

I was here, baby! Watching the whole time.

"Well, that proves you're not a real ghost. You can't be. You didn't even warn me Josh was in there, and you had to know I was heading his way."

A gumshoe gets his facts from watching and keeping his mouth shut, not from crying wolf. Anyway, you were in no danger.

"What do you mean? He just used the women's room mistakenly?"

He didn't "use" it. He was looking for something.

"Looking for what? Tampax tampons?"

Jack laughed. *Thought you didn't like vulgarity.*

"Just spill it!"

Now you're talking my language, baby. Joshy was tearing the ladies' can apart on a search. And he found what he was looking for, too —

"What?"

A syringe — hidden right inside the paper towel dispenser. He pocketed it and took off. Seemed to me, he couldn't get out of here fast enough after he grabbed that needle.

"What was a syringe doing buried in the paper towel dispenser of our women's room?!"

I don't have all the answers yet, but I'll give ya dollars to doughnuts it's got something to do with murder.

"Brennan's?"

Who else you know died in this joint — besides me?

"There could be a perfectly innocent reason why the syringe was hidden in there," I argued.

You don't say? How many hopheads you got in this burg?

"It could have been used for insulin. One of our customers could have been a diabetic."

And the reason he or she shoved it deep inside the towel dispenser instead of into the garbage can?

"I don't know, but —"

No buts. Josh knew what he'd come for. When he'd spotted that syringe, he got the thrills, all right. You'd think he found Veronica Lake naked in his bedroom.

"Please stop with the sexual analogies."

Why, baby? Too much to handle? Am I giving YOU the thrills? That's a nice thought.

143

"What did you say?"

You know what I said. And you know how you feel, hearing my voice in your head.

"Let's stay on the subject at hand. If you're really some all-knowing ghost of a private eye, then what happened to Brennan exactly? Was that syringe involved? And what was it doing in my store's women's room? Who put it there? And what does Josh want with it?"

Whoa. Put the brakes on, baby, I didn't witness who gave Brennan the big chill because I happened to be tailing you that night. And I didn't witness who hid the syringe for the same reason. And as for what Joshy boy wants with it, I can't tail him beyond your front door, so I don't know. I can read your thoughts, but in almost all other ways, my powers of observation are about on your level — with the exception that I can remain invisible, of course, and take in a lot more than you, like that tail I ran on Josh when he was searching the little girls' can. But I can only be one place at a time.

"Forgive me if I remain skeptical."

I don't blame you. But I do need you to pay attention to what I'm telling you now. I have a theory — and a lead for you to follow —

"Oh, no you don't. I'm not doing anything you direct me to until I get a handle on exactly *what* you are."

Suit yourself, baby. When I was alive, I was one skeptic Joe myself. "Concrete Jack" — that's what they used to call me. So if you wanna run

144

your own version of a background check, who am I to complain? Go to it, babe, you have my blessing.

With a dead author, a suspicious State Police investigator, and a hidden syringe in my store over the past twenty-four hours, I was now fairly sure I had a bona fide murder mystery on my hands. And the only one who seemed capable of helping me was a ghost.

Either that or a delusion.

Okay, so the whole "Jack Shepard" matter was a mystery in itself — one I knew I'd better resolve. And fast.

I myself knew next to nothing about ghosts, which meant I needed to consult with experts on the matter — and I needed to do it *anonymously.* That narrowed my investigative options down to one: the Internet.

Chapter 12

Dark and Stormy Night

One of the proofs of the immortality of the soul is that myriads have believed it — they also believed the world was flat.

— Mark Twain

Ghosts are not spirits of the dead. Ghosts don't have innate intelligence. Ghosts are merely the hopes, fears, and emotions of the living, recorded on the psychic plane and replayed in an eternal, endless loop long after the person who inadvertently made that recording is dead.

Such was the hypothesis of Dr. Frederic Haxan, author and paranormal researcher, as typed in a message to me by a graduate student with the self-explanatory screen name SPOOKSCIENCEGUY.

For the past hour I had fruitlessly surfed the cyberwaves, using the keywords "ghosts" and "haunting." After hopping from one search engine to another, and one crackpot Web site to another, I'd finally stumbled onto this site, sponsored by the Department of Parapsychology at Wendell University (wherever that was).

I entered their active chat room and met SPOOKSCIENCEGUY, KARDECIAN, DOYLEFAIRY, M. BLAVATSKY, and the rest of the "Ghostbusters."

At last, I could talk freely about my problem. I mean, honestly, how could I tell anyone that I was having an ongoing conversation in my head with the voice of a dead private eye? They were sure to assume I was suffering some sort of post-traumatic stress from witnessing my late husband's leap.

Going to a doctor was out for the same reason. Diagnosis of nut job might land me in a straitjacket. And forget my in-laws, that's all the excuse they'd need to take Spencer away from me for good.

I took a long sip from my mug of lukewarm coffee and shifted my gaze from the flickering computer screen to the dark, rain-swept street. An SUV swished by, splashing water on the soggy curb, then the thunder rumbled in the distance, and I imagined storm clouds gathering miles off Narragansett Bay, brooding over the surface of the ocean.

Okay, so "dark and stormy night" is a total cliché, but it really *was* such a night. And there I sat alone, behind Buy the Book's checkout counter, typing away on an Internet chat room, reading supernatural jargon from a gaggle of parapsychologists.

I was about to pose a question to SPOOKSCIENCEGUY — one of the thirteen people now chatting — when screen name DOYLEFAIRY crashed our conversation.

"SPOOKSCIEGUY, YOU ARE FULL OF POO-DOO,"

wrote DOYLEFAIRY in big, bold, irritated letters.

"The 1957 Pevensey Castle incident proved ghosts do not exist. The psychic phenomena attributed to specters are really the work of elves and fairies."

Elves and fairies!?! I suddenly wondered what planet or dimensional plane DOYLE-FAIRY hailed from.

"Way off base, FAIRY,"

screen name VENKMANN flashed a moment later.

"The Pevensey Castle photos are a hoax. That whole incident is about as real as the Cardiff Giant."

GHOSTHUNTER jumped into the fray, followed quickly by COLDSPOT, WENDIGO, and GHOUL-LISHOUS.

I sat back and watched the argument scroll down my computer screen through bleary eyes, my too-fuzzy brain trying to make some sense of what these participants in the *wendellunv.edu/psyphenom/talk* chat room were saying.

Terms like "manifestations," "elementals," "poltergeist," "exteriorization phenomena," and "ur-spirits" were flying — most of them landing somewhere over my head. Meanwhile, the patter of rain against the arched front window was lulling me to sleep.

I blinked my eyes. My computer monitor began to flicker, and the sound of the rain receded. Against the scrolling banter of chat room text, I saw a man's powerful profile. Jaw square. Fedora pulled low over the eyes.

I jumped, fully awake now. The vision vanished. Onscreen, the debate continued about my topic: sudden visitations from an outspoken ghost.

GHOSTHUNTER suggested an explanation for my "friend's" problem. (Yes, I tried that transparent ploy, and no one who responded to my questions even pretended my "friend" was anyone but me — evidenced by the fact that they always put quote marks around the word "friend.")

GHOSTHUNTER said my "friend" might be experiencing a form of demonic possession. This theory was predicated on the evidence that my "friend" was the only person to hear the entity, witness its physical manifestations, and its evil trickery (the upside-down chairs).

GHOSTHUNTER even had two suggestions: read Malachi Martin's *Hostage to the Devil,* and see *The Exorcist.*

Gee, what a comfort.

DOYLEFAIRY conveyed that "exteriorization phenomena" like turning over chairs and turning them back again was more indicative of poltergeist activity — none too subtly adding that poltergeists, though known as "mischievous spirits," could be far more dangerous than the definition suggested — the word "mischievous" connoting, to me anyway, the sorts of things one might see the Peanuts gang doing in a Sunday comic strip.

DOYLEFAIRY also suggested that some "hysterical female" in our household was partly to blame because poltergeist activity required human energy to perform their antics. An anxious adolescent girl might provide such energy — or a mentally unstable woman of childbearing age, in some cases.

How nice, I thought, to be informed that I was mentally unstable by a woman who believed in elves and fairies.

I was getting increasingly frustrated. If these parapsychologists were any indication, then the "experts" in the field couldn't even agree on the definition of the word "ghost." How were they going to help me with my "dilemma"? (I will also confess that I seriously began to wonder if I needed to be a Roman Catholic to summon an exorcist.)

Suddenly, a newcomer joined the chat room: WANNADATE. "I've got huge breasts and a tiny skirt, and I'm looking for friendship."

What the heck was that? I thought, supremely alarmed. But before I could type a thing, the entire chat room told WANNADATE to take a hike.

Major obscenities came across my screen before the chat room moderator ejected WANNADATE from the group.

"Who in the world was that?"

I typed.

"Sorry, HAUNTED,"

SPOOKSCIENCEGUY typed back to me,

"every now and then some jerk gets our address and crashes."

"No problem,"

I typed.

". . . but elves and fairies are considered elemental spirits,"

DOYLEFAIRY was now typing, amid some sort of parapsychological argument with KARDECIAN.

Okay, I thought. I'll bite.

"Excuse me, but what is an 'elemental' spirit?"

I typed.

"A spirit of the earth,"

typed DOYLEFAIRY.

"They only exist if people believe in them."

"Oh, come on,"

I typed, unable to stop myself.

"Like Tinkerbell?"

"Actually, that's not a bad example at all,"

typed DOYLEFAIRY, apparently unruffled by my apparent skepticism. (Then again, if you professed to believe in fairies, you'd have to get a pretty thick skin, wouldn't you?)

"Just consider how J. M. Barrie laid it out,"

typed DOYLEFAIRY.

"He posited that saving Tinkerbell's life, after she drinks the poison meant for Peter Pan, could be achieved by asking everyone to profess their belief in fairies. Accurate. Even though that was an example drawn from literature, there are historical and cultural examples like it. The leprechauns of Ireland, for instance."

Okay, I thought, I'll bite again.

"So, if belief in these elemental spirits is what keeps them alive, then what happens if people stop believing in them?"

DOYLEFAIRY typed,

"I can use Peter Pan again for that one. Just stating the words 'I don't believe in fairies' supposedly results in some fairy somewhere in the world dropping dead on the spot. That's pretty much it. Once people stop believing in these elemental spirits, their psychic energies are dispersed."

I asked, "You mean they go away?"

"Yes. The psychic energy disperses and collects elsewhere."

Elsewhere, I thought. Like where? But what I typed was,

"Then all I have to do is tell my friend to ignore the ghost."

I was momentarily caught up with the thrill of an easy answer. Completely ignoring the ghost of Jack Shepard could be a no-fuss, no-muss way to end all of this. All I needed was a big, fat YES.

"No!"

typed GHOSTHUNTER almost instantly.

"No, no, no! Ghosts are not fairies, for heaven's sake. Ghosts are the souls of those whose bodies have died. Contrary to the Haxan hypotheses, which SPOOK-SCIENCEGUY quoted for you, many parapsychologists believe ghosts exhibit an independent personality. There are many documented accounts of ghosts communicating things to the living that the living didn't previously know."

Darn, I thought. Darn, darn, darn.

"We have more than one hundred of these kinds of stories in our files,"

typed GHOSTHUNTER.

"And those are just the ones reported to

154

us. Most of the time, supernatural en-
counters are so private or unverifiable,
people decide to keep them to themselves
rather than risk sounding — you know —
crazy."

I typed,

"Believe me, I know."

As the data stream went on, I let the chat
room continue and opened up a second Web
window to surf an on-line bookstore for titles
relating to mental diseases, delusions, de-
mentia, and nervous breakdowns. The title *A
Beautiful Mind* popped up, and I felt slightly
better. After all, if a Nobel Prize–winning
mathematician could learn to live with
hearing delusional voices, maybe I could, too.
Sorry, babe, Jack Shepard said. *Sorry to give
you the grouch, but I am really not a delusion.
Really.*
I sighed. If Jack Shepard's spirit was only a
voice in my head, as it had been for Professor John Nash, then I would have to start
establishing some limits right now!
"I want to be alone," I said in a clear
voice.
That seemed to work. The ghost had decided not to press the point.
I stifled a yawn and was about to sign off
when screen name RUNE flashed me a pri-

vate "INSTANT MESSAGE."

"You seem to have more than an academic interest in psychic phenomena,"

the message read.

I remembered seeing the name RUNE on the chat list, but I did not recall that name participating in the discussion. After a long pause, another instant message appeared.

"I can understand if you don't wish to share your issues with me privately,"

the message read.

"Though I am sure they are preying upon you."

I typed a bland reply, something like

"You don't know the half of it."

Then I pressed the "send" button.
Only after the reply came did I realize I had been holding my breath waiting for it.

"Just consider this,"

said RUNE.

"Psychic talents are like any other talent. As children we are all psychic to some degree. But without an environment to practice and develop our skills, we never know our true potential. Some of us even bury our talent as we mature only to have it crop up in odd ways."

"Crop up? How?"

I typed.

"The answer to that depends on the individual. But this I know: Once you've learned to talk to the dead, you never forget how."

"What does that mean?"

I typed.

"Are you saying that I should just go ahead"

— I stopped typing, hit the backspace to delete, and began typing again —

"that I should tell my friend to just go ahead and start talking to this — ghost?"

"I know you're skeptical. But look, if you — that is, your 'friend' "

— typed RUNE,

"doesn't believe in ghosts, then why not think of it as an alter ego, a part of the secret self trying to break through with a message? Why not 'dialogue' with it and see where it might lead?"

I thought of Calvin. *Splat.* Not a pretty picture.

"The unknown is a scary place, isn't it?"

typed RUNE when I didn't answer for a full minute.

"Very,"

I typed back.

You think this is a lot of supernatural baloney, don't you? said the voice of Jack loud and clear in my head.

Onscreen, RUNE instant-messaged once more before signing off from the chat list.

"Supernatural. Perhaps. Baloney? Definitely not. After all, why do you think it's called an after*life*?"

"This is crazy, all right," I muttered. "And maybe I am, too."

Chapter 13

Don't Know Jack

The chief problem about death . . . is the fear that there may be no afterlife, a depressing thought, particularly for those who have bothered to shave. . . . I do not believe in an afterlife, although I am bringing a change of underwear.

— Woody Allen

Jack watched Penelope log off the supernatural chat room site and begin frantically searching for information on what she assumed was her "mental condition."

"Online Psychological Testing . . ." she mumbled, reading the screen. "Addictions, Anxiety, Bipolar Disorder . . . no, no, no. . . ."

Funny thing, the computer, thought Jack. Before Penelope, he hadn't given the boxy typewriter two looks. For one thing, it appeared a cold, remote medium, like his old office's Underwood. Every now and again, Jack would notice the screen above the keyboard reading "Inventory" or "Account Orders," and Sadie typing away with a glassy-eyed look that reminded him of his old gum-chewing secretary.

(Not a bad-looking dame, his secretary, but not his type — that is, not much upstairs, which was actually why Jack had hired her. She had no interest in getting wise to his clients' secrets or Jack's. Just typed, filed, and answered phones, which was what he needed. In the end, the private dick business came with enough female distractions on the job as it was. Why compound that interest?)

Anyhow, in old Aunt Sadie's hands, the computer seemed like little more than a type-writer. But not in Penelope's. With that sharp cookie at the wheel, that plastic box had come alive, racing down alleyways he'd never even known existed.

Take that gab-room thing. Ten people all over the world spilling guts and squaring beefs, one after the other, faster than a bookie giving odds at post time. (Even though some of them did remind Jack of those uptown hustlers, full of gin and big words.)

And those information searches the doll was doing right now. Answers to all sorts of questions with the stroke of a few keys. People, places, events. It spun Jack like a top.

If he had a nickel for all the shoe leather he'd worn out tracking down information for just one case, he'd have died a rich man.

In fact, it seemed to Jack this new century had enough ready gadgets to make it possible for your average housewife to become a private dick — which reminded Jack of why he needed to talk to Penelope tonight in the first place: Brennan's murder. And that syringe Josh had swiped.

"Depression . . ." murmured Penelope, staring at the "Psych Subjects" screen for a long moment. She clicked on the glowing blue D-word and the green screen dissolved into a white page with large black type at the top: CLINICAL DEPRESSION SCREENING TEST.

Because Penelope was nearsighted, she'd removed the black rectangular frames when she'd first sat down to read the computer screen, giving Jack a rare glimpse of her naked face.

The light from the computer screen reflected in her eyes, burnishing the copper irises with tiny flecks of buried gold and making her pale skin appear smooth as cream. With her lips slightly swollen from her nervous gnawing, and her reddish-brown hair mussed, Jack thought she looked as though she'd just risen from a night of lovemaking.

What he wouldn't give to occupy a body again for just a few hours. He'd pull her up, out of that chair, into his arms. What he wouldn't give to feel his hardness against her softness . . .

"This is a self-assessment test presented by mentalhealth.com," Penelope murmured. "Please click the boxes that apply to you:

Feelings of sadness and/or irritability. Check. Loss of interest or pleasure in activities once enjoyed. Check. Difficulty getting out of bed. Check. Inability to concentrate, work, or make decisions. Definitely a check —"

Waste of time, doll, Jack interrupted. *You're not depressed.*

Penelope's fingers stilled over the keyboard. Her body stiffened the way it always did when he penetrated her mind.

Well? Jack asked. *Didn't your chat room friend . . . RUNE . . . didn't RUNE advise you to "dialogue" with me?*

"I'm not sure it's a good idea to take psychological advice from a person who professes to believe in ghosts."

Aw, shucks, doll, said Jack. *You don't believe in me? You want me to provide you a mental projection again, like I did last night?*

"Is that what I saw?" Penelope whispered. "A mental projection?"

Don't know what else to call it, said Jack.

"How about a hallucination?"

What a pill, Jack thought to himself. Okay, baby. Time to play hardball.

Turn off the lights again, he told her with the equivalent of a low rasp in her ear. He swirled himself silently around her, taking pleasure in the way goose bumps formed on the surface of her skin, and her ample breasts rose and fell with quickening breaths. *I dare you . . .*

"No!" Penelope said, even as shivers ran through her, giving her the startling revelation that he could manifest signs of his physical presence. "I can't feel you. I can't."

You can. It's me. He breezed by her again, and again she shivered, shutting her pretty copper eyes, the dark lashes brushing her pale cheeks in a way that made Jack even more restless.

"You go away now," she said.

Jack laughed.

"I mean it."

He laughed again.

Penelope stood up, her small hands balling into fists. She released a breath, then opened her eyes and grabbed up her clunky black glasses, shoving them on her face like armor.

"Get out of my head!" she cried. "Get out of my store!"

Calm down, baby. You're in no danger. At least not yet — and I'm only bothering you now because I'd like to keep it that way for you and yours. Get me?

Jack backed away, letting the air around her warm again. Penelope took a deep breath. "You're trying to *protect* me? And my family?"

Ready to open an eardrum now?

"Fine," she said, sinking slowly back into her chair. "Proceed."

First let's get some things out of the way. I can't stand it when broads pretend I'm not wise to things. It's time to put the cards on the table. I want you to know what I know about you.

"What do you know about me?"

Everything. You're a widow, that's easy, but you haven't let a living soul know how you really felt about your husband. Maybe not even yourself.

"Okay, I'll bite. How do I feel?"

You didn't love him.

"How dare you —"

Save the energy, doll. Hubby leaped from an Upper East Side high-rise. You even glimpsed the guy taking the big plunge when you opened the bedroom door unexpectedly. And, after the initial shock over the man's sad end, you felt mainly one thing: worry for your son's well-being. And that was it. You're sorry for the way he died, but you don't miss him in the least.

"I won't dignify that with an answer."

Don't. We both know it's true. And we both know why.

"Oh, WE both know, do we?"

You were trying to raise a little boy with dragon-hearted in-laws breathing down your neck, and your mealy-mouthed man giving you a manifesto that read something like he found fatherhood a bore. How'm I doing?

Penelope sat very still.

He stopped sleeping with you, too, Jack continued. *And no matter what you did, what you said to try to help him, or get him help, the sap refused to make the least bit of effort to find a*

164

way out of the well. That is, until he took the cloward's way out. Or should I say down. All the way to the bottom and six feet under. That about cover it?

After a long pause, Penelope whispered, "It's all true. Yes."

So that clinical depression checklist you're going through isn't for you, is it?

"No."

It's for Calvin, right?

"I should have done it when it mattered. For a solid month he told me he was looking for a better therapist, that his old one was a quack. He kept telling me he was taking his medicine."

But he wasn't. On either count.

"That's right. And he was —"

Get it out, sister.

"Weak. Calvin was weak, which meant he could also be mean. He never struck me, but when he didn't get his way, he could be abusive . . . verbally abusive."

So you distanced yourself.

"That's a nice way of putting it. What I did was give up on him . . . and the truth is I was close to leaving him."

But he left you first.

"Yes."

So you blame yourself.

"Of course I blame myself. I was his wife."

Listen, I got a story for you, one of my cases. A wife comes in one day to hire me as a tail for her husband. Pretty little thing. Had a baby at home. Said her husband was an alkie. He'd have a bad week, get bombed on Friday, sleep with whatever had a pulse, then drag home again about Sunday. Swear he'd never do it again. Promised he'd get help to kick the booze. The week would go by. Come Friday, he was in the bar, knocking them back. So . . . what do you think?

"What do I think? Of what?"

Of the wife? How many years should the authorities have put her in prison for . . . I mean for the terrible crime of not getting her husband to sober up and stop treating her like dirt?

"It wasn't the wife's fault."

My point exactly, doll.

"No. My situation was not the same as hers. Calvin was sick. He was depressed. I know back in your time, society didn't recognize depression as a disease — alcoholism, either, for that matter. But these things are sicknesses. People can't kick them on their own. They need help."

Which you tell me you tried to get him. But he refused.

"I could have committed him."

Would his family have let you?

"Probably not. They didn't see Calvin the way I did. He showed them a different face, and he'd never said anything about suicide — not to me, anyway. He'd even rallied the week before. Started organizing things, seemed more upbeat."

You didn't PUSH him out the window, did you?

"No, of course not. Although sometimes the way his family looks at me — I think they wonder if I did."

Screw them. Him, too. And I don't mean maybe, baby, he's the one that bailed. All that counts now is you and your son. You're in it together. Isn't that what you told the kid this morning?

There was a long pause. "You were there this morning? With us? In Spencer's room? You heard me say that?"

So anyway, sugar, let's get back to that syringe in your ladies' —

"Oh, no you don't. I want you to answer my question. Were you spying on us? On me? Upstairs in our private rooms?"

I like to think of it as surveillance.

"Well, I forbid you to go up there again."

Lady, you can't lay down house rules to a man with no body.

"I can so! I can ask you to promise not to haunt the second floor, on your honor as a . . . as a spirit."

Forget it.

"You know you're being unreasonable, Jack."

Another long pause ensued.

"Jack?"

That's the first time you called me by my name.

Penelope bit her lip. "Sorry."

No, no, it's all right by me. Jack breezed close again. *I liked hearing you say it.*

Penelope gave a little shiver. "Let's get back to that business of Josh," she said. "What would he want with a hidden syringe?"

Here's my theory: That syringe was used to poison Brennan in some way last night. Now, the killer would have been crazy to keep it on her because she couldn't bet the police wouldn't search the people in attendance in some way. And she wouldn't throw it in the trash because that's exactly where the cops would look first — and the State Police did cart last night's trash away, didn't they?

"Yes, they did. But why do you keep saying 'her' and 'she'? How can you be sure the killer was a woman?"

Because a man going into the ladies' can on the night Brennan keeled would have raised immediate alarms. A man would have hidden it in the men's room. The person you're looking for has to be a woman — at least as far as hiding the syringe goes. Doesn't necessarily mean she's the actual killer. She could simply be an accomplice, working with a man or another woman.

"I'm with you. Go on."

The woman would have hid it in your ladies' john, hoping to return for it another day.

"Or she might have paid someone to retrieve it for her. Someone like Josh."

It's possible. But wouldn't she have told Josh exactly where to find the syringe, instead of making him search for it and risk getting caught?

"Well, if Josh wasn't hired to find the syringe, then why was he looking for it in the first place?"

Don't know.

"What do you mean, you don't know? Didn't you read his thoughts?"

Couldn't.

"But you've been reading mine."

Told you before, I can only read yours. Get it through your head, babe, I'm not some kind of all-knowing divine spirit. I'm just a dead dick.

"All right. I get it. So what should I do now?"

Narrow down your suspect list. Josh is suspect number one. But he had to search for that syringe, which means he wasn't the one to plant it — so who did?

"Deirdre?"

Possibly. She has the best motive. You yourself heard her say she had no love for Daddy dearest. And she's inheriting all his loot.

"I'm sure that's what Lieutenant Marsh will conclude."

Who else?

"Her husband, Kenneth Franken?"

They could be in it together. Who else?

"Deirdre said Brennan was about to divorce

his third wife. Maybe she tried something."

Wouldn't Deirdre or Brennan have recognized Brennan's wife at the event last night?

"Oh, yes, that's right. They would have."

She could have hired someone, though — a doll willing to do the dirty deed. And there could be other suspects with motives we just haven't uncovered yet.

"What about Shelby Cabot? Josh reports to her. So it makes sense he'd do a favor for her like retrieve the syringe. But what motive could she have? Unless she was hired by Brennan's wife."

It's a long shot. So far Deirdre and you look like the prime suspects.

"Me?!"

Don't act so shocked, doll; you said it yourself earlier. You're benefiting from the murder, aren't you? You and Sadie.

"The police haven't called it a murder yet."

But you know they think there's foul play. They're just waiting for the medical examiner to give them the toxicology evidence before they make their arrest.

Penelope took a deep breath. "Then what do I do next?"

Suddenly a *tap, tap, tapping* sounded on the store's arched front window, and Penelope nearly jumped out of her skin. Jack didn't have any skin, but the vibrations startled him, too.

Looks like you've got a visitor, said Jack. *And*

170

a late one at that. So here's my professional, ex-
pert opinion about what to do next —

"What?"

Answer the door.

Chapter 14

Strangers in the Night

Somebody was nuts. I was nuts. Everybody was nuts.
None of it fitted together worth a nickel.
— Philip Marlowe, "Trouble Is My Business" by Raymond Chandler, *Dime Detective magazine*, August 1939

Outside in the darkness, a trench-coated figure stood beyond the bookstore's rain-splattered window. An open umbrella, tilted at an angle, masked the face.

"Who is it?" I whispered to Jack.

How should I know? I'm a spirit, not a psychic.

Tap, tap, tap went the person at the window once more. I stepped around the counter and into a cone of light cast by the ceiling fixtures. The big black umbrella moved, and I recognized the pretty pert face and short, shiny, raven hair of Shelby Cabot, the publicist from Salient House. She caught sight of me and waved.

"What should I say to her?" I whispered to Jack. "I mean, to get her to say what she might know about Josh and Deirdre and Kenneth?"

Just get her talking. About anything. Then turn the conversation where you want it, so she doesn't get wise to being grilled.

"Okay," I murmured, "wish me luck."

Baby, you don't need luck in this profession. What you need is brains, and you got plenty, so go to it.

I unbolted the door, and Shelby stepped in. "I know it's late, Mrs. McClure," she said as she shook the large umbrella, dripping water all over my newly restored plank floor. "I was strolling by the store and saw the lights on and, well —"

"Uh-huh," I replied, frankly dubious that anyone would be "strolling by" on a night like this one.

Shelby pulled off her sopping raincoat and draped it over a nearby Shaker-style rocker. Dribbling water puddled in the cross-hatched seat.

"I heard sales were brisk today," she said.

"Oh, yes."

"How wonderful!" she exclaimed, though her forced grin gave me the impression she didn't care in the least.

I turned to bolt the door, but something caught my attention: a man was loitering across the street, just beyond the dull beams of the streetlight on the corner. In my head, I whispered to Jack, "Who is that standing across the street?"

How should I know? he said.

"What kind of response is that?! You're supposed to be a private eye. Go on over and find out!"

Can't leave the premises, doll. Don't ask me why.

"Why?"

Because I don't have an answer.

Frustrated with Jack's double-talk, I stared harder beyond the door's pane, trying to make out the details of the dark silhouette, but I didn't recognize the rain slicker, and the big hood was pulled up and around the man's face.

I'd been peering through the window so intensely, I nearly jumped when Shelby spoke up behind me: "I don't suppose you received that special order yet? The one I had sent directly from our warehouse?"

I turned to face her, noticing the woman's gaze was not on me at all. She'd been looking at the figure across the street, too. When I answered, however, she immediately shifted her eyes to me.

"Actually, five hundred hardcovers arrived this morning," I said.

"Isn't it convenient the Salient House warehouse is just an hour away," said Shelby. "Normally, an order like that would take much longer to fulfill."

"Yes, I was surprised by the speed — but I

was absolutely shocked by the amount of books in the order. I mean, last night, you said 'a few' more books would be charged to our account number. I can't figure where 'a few' translates into twenty cartons."

"Of course, Salient House will accept any returns —"

"To tell you the truth, when the delivery man rolled all of those boxes in this morning, I feared we'd never move so many copies. But we've already sold more than half the shipment. It turns out you were right to order so many."

"I'm so glad," Shelby replied. "I could see from the way you'd mismanaged the event room setup last night that you wouldn't be on top of your inventory needs, either."

Did she just take a shot at me? I wondered.

She aimed and fired, all right, Jack said in my head.

"Well, as new releases go, I can't say that I have any experience managing inventory for a circumstance like this one," I said politely, evading an accusation that her large order did force us into a position where we appeared to be *exploiting* an author's sudden death.

The implication didn't seem to bother Shelby in the least. "Of course, it's understandable how the whole thing was just beyond your abilities to handle," she answered breezily. "Isn't it fortuitous the way it all turned out — that I was able to do the right thing for you and your store? At Salient House, we're often exasperated by the provincial attitudes of our unsophisticated vendors, especially those independent booksellers not based in major urban areas. So many such booksellers just aren't willing to take full advantage of a *situation*."

In typical "corporate speak" — polite, evasive, and nonspecific — I *guess* the tragedy of Timothy Brennan's death could be called a "situation."

"This store *is* impressive," Shelby said, moving suddenly from insulting to ingratiating. "And *such* a responsibility."

"We try," I said.

"Well, don't feel bad about not knowing quite enough about the publishing business yet." Shelby Cabot's eyes locked on mine. "Just as long as you rely on the help of people like me."

Was this woman actually *trying* to provoke me? I wondered.

If you're gonna imitate a doormat, Jack barked in my head, *the least you could do is stretch out on the floor so she can wipe her feet.*

"I admit, Mr. Brennan's signing was this store's very first," I said. "But I have had plenty of experience in the publishing business."

"Really?" Shelby replied. She arched an

eyebrow skeptically, even as she brushed a wet ringlet of black hair away from her high, smooth forehead.

"Oh, yes," I continued, naming the publisher I had worked for, and a brace of popular authors with whom I'd worked in my days as a "publishing professional."

As I rattled off the names, I realized it *was* an impressive list, even if my dealings with some of those talents would be casually dismissed as "past history" — because, unfortunately, these days publishing operated on the "What have you done for me lately?" principle. The key, of course, being the post-dot-bomb era's interpretation of the word "lately," which used to mean over the past five years, but now meant over the past six weeks (the length of time chain stores gave a book to catch on before it was sent back to the publisher's warehouse in a DDS truck).

Unfortunately, by the time I was finished reciting my résumé, I felt cheap and hollow. Suddenly I was having a flashback to my worst days in that badly managed New York publishing office, where the overall dynamic was vintage John Bradshaw dysfunctional family.

In my experience, lazy, bad managers were the ones most impressed by the slick self-promoters. The hardest workers, who tended to be boring nose-to-the-grindstone types, were subsequently overlooked. My problem was that I'd been brought up to believe self-promotion was *not*, in fact, a virtue. Bragging, I'd been taught, was a form of conceit not to be encouraged, respected, or admired. And it's something I still believe, frankly.

However, when the vulgar endeavor of blowing your own horn becomes the quickest road to advancement in an office, you're sunk if you keep your mouth shut.

Style over substance, lip service over true service, self-promotion for rank promotion: I shudder to think how many offices in America are managed with this philosophy. But, I fear, it's an inescapable reality. Thus, boring, dedicated workers go unrewarded — while slick, pushy operators are put in charge.

I actually felt my stomach turn as these memories of office politics washed over me. I wanted to believe I was over all this, that I'd put it firmly behind me with my move north. But Shelby had dragged me right back, down to her level. A few minor insults and I'd stooped to bragging in my own defense.

Don't be so hard on yourself, said Jack. *I got dragged down plenty in back alleys. Sometime there's nothing you can do about it. Just make sure your punches land.*

Okay, maybe I did land a good one: Shelby's smile became a little more plastic, a little more forced, and I felt that sickly familiar sense of satisfaction. But my victory was fleeting. Women like Shelby were far better than I at this game.

"Interesting bit of experience you've had," she snipped with the sort of creepy cheeriness one usually only hears in a gothic melodrama. "Too bad it's all behind you. Don't feel too bad about it, though. Not everyone can hack the big leagues."

My fantasy about wringing her neck was interrupted, thankfully, by my own private dick. *You've done a good job distracting her, doll. Now ask about Joshy boy.*

Jack was right, of course — and he probably noticed that I'd done a good job distracting *myself*, too. Okay, I thought, back to business.

"It's so very difficult to decide about people," I said, trying hard to keep my delivery casual. "I mean, it takes a truly gifted manager to quickly judge who has the 'right stuff' and who is just going to be some total loser, you know? To judge right away who deserves your encouragement and help and who you should crush — for the good of the company, of course."

"That's *very* true." Shelby's eyes widened with glee.

Bingo! People like Shelby were fairly transparent. Nailing her "philosophy" on office politics wasn't hard.

"I wonder, what's your opinion of someone

like *Josh?*" I asked. "Do you think *he'll* make it?"

She flapped her hand. "Josh is a conniving little toady, if you want my unvarnished opinion."

"Oh, by all means. Don't hold back."

"It's nothing personal. I like him otherwise, you understand. He's just typical of the kids coming out of college these days. Doesn't want to listen to people above him — just wants responsibility handed to him. Like this very hot literary author the company's putting on tour in January. Josh has got it in his head that he can direct the tour, take care of the author, and handle all the media appearances. Crazy. He's been with the company less than a year, and he's already lobbying me for a prime assignment like that. But I don't trust him, frankly. And I think he'd do just about anything to get ahead."

That gave me pause.

Okay, so I didn't like Shelby, but I believed what she was saying where Josh was concerned — mainly because her summation was rapid-fire and not in the least forced. There was no sign of the plastic expressions or ingratiating fakeness of her previous exchanges. Nothing phony was present in her judgment of Josh; she'd meant what she'd said.

And what does that tell you? asked Jack.

"It tells me that Josh has a motive for doing something risky, like helping Brennan's killer," I silently told Jack, "*if* the risk helps him advance his career. But I don't see any connection between Brennan's death and Josh's advancement. Unless he's helping Shelby, and she's the killer, but what motive would she have for killing Brennan? Her glory was in directing his big book tour — and now that's over. Shelby had no motive to kill Brennan. None that I can see."

There's got to be a connection between Josh and the murderer. You just need to find more dots to connect, doll. So look for more dots.

I was about to ask Shelby more about Josh when I heard footsteps outside. I turned to see a hooded figure lunging toward the door.

I screamed. Shelby Cabot screamed. And the figure recoiled back.

Then he lunged forward again and jiggled the door handle, but found it locked.

"Who is it?" I cried. "Who are you?"

The man pulled down the hood of his L.L.Bean rain slicker and pointed to the handle of the locked door.

"It's Kenneth!" Shelby said to me. "Kenneth Franken."

I looked again. It *was* Kenneth Franken, the late Timothy Brennan's son-in-law — though right now, with his soaked-through rain slicker and drooping hair, he more resembled a half-drowned lobsterman just finished with his traps.

I unbolted the door. As Kenneth stepped

in, the downpour followed him. Rain splattered everywhere.

"I'm sorry I frightened you," he said.

"Come in and get dry," I told him.

As he came through the doorway, Kenneth slipped on the wet floor and grabbed my arm to steady himself.

"Excuse me," he mumbled.

Kenneth Franken's hand was cold — very cold, and he was soaked to the skin. Obviously, he had been out in the night a long time. I glanced across the street, but that loitering man was gone. I knew then that he had been that man.

How odd, I thought. Why would Franken lurk about in the rain? Why not just knock?

Franken turned to stare at Shelby Cabot. The woman wheeled, deliberately giving him her back, which Kenneth just stared at. So I stood staring at Kenneth. The silence continued until I, for one, was feeling rather embarrassed. I was about to say something to break the obvious tension when Shelby turned around and faced me.

"I am sorry to trouble you," she said, running her hand through her wet hair. "But could I . . . freshen up somewhere?"

"Certainly," I said, although her still-flawless makeup seemed *Titanic* proof to me.

"Upstairs?" she asked, gesturing.

"No. We have rest rooms on this level, beyond the events area near the emergency exit."

Shelby Cabot nodded and walked off.

When she was out of earshot, Kenneth Franken spoke.

"I'm sorry about my behavior earlier today," he began. "Getting so upset about the makeup case. With my wife so distraught, I've been under a strain. You understand, don't you?"

"Of course I understand."

"Good, good . . . uhm . . . yes . . . well . . . I came by tonight because" — he looked at the floor, then at the shelves, then off in the direction where Shelby had gone — "I was wondering if you knew anything at all about what my late father-in-law announced last evening. The matter about the real Jack Shepard disappearing in this town, maybe on these premises."

Call me crazy, but it seemed awfully late for him to suddenly come by just to ask a question like that. He'd been here hours ago and hadn't mentioned a thing about it.

Nevertheless, he'd asked me a direct question, so I searched my mind, sorting through my past experiences growing up in this town. I thought about Aunt Sadie, who'd inherited the store from her father, who'd inherited the store from his brother — a mysterious figure in the family whom I knew very little about.

The fact was, for this question, I'd need some help.

"Jack?" I said aloud, hoping the ghost

would silently supply me some facts. But he clearly wasn't offering any details at the moment.

"Yes, Jack Shepard," said Kenneth, who assumed, of course, I had spoken to him.

"I'm sorry," I said after a long pause — and complete silence from my ghost. "I really don't know what Mr. Brennan was talking about. Of course, you could come back tomorrow and ask my aunt. Sadie's memory reaches a lot farther back than mine."

"Perhaps I shall. I do apologize for coming here so late, but I wanted to speak in private. There were so many people around today — you do understand?"

"Yes, of course," I replied, feeling like he was trying awfully hard to make me *not* suspect him of anything, which, of course, made me certain he was guilty of *something*. "You're welcome to come by anytime, Mr. Franken."

"Thank you. . . ."

He paused, seeing Shelby Cabot emerge from the shadows of the events room. Her hair was combed, her makeup still perfect, but she didn't seem noticeably "fresher"; in fact, she seemed more pale, more tense than before.

"I think we've troubled Mrs. McClure long enough for one evening," Kenneth said. Then he handed Shelby her coat. "*We* should really be going now."

The emphasis was on "we," and despite the

fact that Shelby Cabot looked like she wished to remain, good manners forced her to say good night.

"I'll see you again, Mr. Franken?" I asked as neutrally as possible.

"Oh, yes," he replied. "Detective-Lieutenant Marsh asked my wife and me to stay on for a few days . . . answer any questions that might arise . . . that sort of thing. And you know Deirdre wants to hold a press conference here — when the state medical examiner's office releases their autopsy findings."

"Oh, yes, that's right. Well, good night, then," I said. I opened the door and ushered the pair into the night.

Immediately, I spoke to the air. "Jack, hurry and follow them."

Can't.

"What do you mean, 'can't'?"

Through the window, I watched Shelby and Kenneth walk slowly down Cranberry Street, in the direction of Quindicott Pond and Finch's Inn, which made sense, since they were both checked in there. Suddenly they stopped and began to argue.

"Come on, Jack, get a move on! Get out there!"

Penelope, listen to me. I can't get beyond the walls and windows of this store. Believe me, doll, I would if I could. There're plenty of places hipper than this cornball town.

185

"I don't understand. Why don't you just try?"

I have tried.

"And? What happens?"

Have you ever tried breathing on the bottom of the ocean? It's like that for me, honey. Water, water everywhere — and I'm no fish. That's how all-powerful I am. Getting noplace fast, and this joint's my life raft . . . so to speak.

"Great."

So, doll, you're the one who's gonna tail them.

"Me?!"

You saw it yourself. Shelby Cabot and Kenneth Franken behaved like they had something to hide. And a little eavesdropping will probably tell you what pretty quick. So get going.

"Jack, I don't know —"

Don't go limp on me now, baby. They know something. And the state's suspect list could easily have your name on it, so you better get tough and get going. Your marks are going to be gone in a few.

"Crap!"

I hurried to the top of the stairs, where wooden pegs held the family coats. Instead of my traditional canary-yellow slicker, I reached for Sadie's slate gray fisherman's coat with a wide-brimmed hood — outerwear designed to stand up against stiff nor'easters. My choice was not guided by the weather, however. I needed the camouflage.

Down the stairs and out the door, I caught

sight of my "marks" ahead of me on Cranberry Street. Kenneth and Shelby were slowly moving through the drenching rain, their silhouettes outlined by a nearby streetlight.

The air was raw. Gusts of chilly wind blew the pelting rain up under my hood, spattering drops against my face and dewing my black-framed glasses.

I walked at a brisk pace, though it took only a few steps to determine that my low-heeled shoes weren't nearly as weather-resistant as my outerwear. In only a moment my feet became soaking wet. Fortunately, the wind and the rain were loud enough to muffle the sound of my footsteps as I began to catch up to Shelby and Kenneth.

"Is this how you tailed 'marks' when you were a detective, Jack?" I asked to dispel my nervousness. But before I even finished the question, I knew he wouldn't reply.

I wanted to believe he'd lied to me, that he'd played me just to get me out here on a tail, but the gaping feeling of emptiness told me he'd been truthful. A void seemed to open up inside me, and I suddenly felt very alone.

"I wish you were here, Jack Shepard," I murmured.

By now I was close enough to hear Kenneth's and Shelby's voices, though I couldn't quite make out the words. They were agitated; that much was obvious. At one point,

Kenneth reached out and grabbed Shelby's elbow. He tried to push her forward, but she yanked her arm free. I dared to move a little closer.

"Brennan was a bastard . . ." I heard Kenneth say, his tone bitter. "He stood in the way . . ."

The rest of his words were lost in the downpour. Luckily the pair paused at the corner and faced one another. I moved closer, aware that darkness and rain were my only covers.

"Are you sorry you did it?" Shelby asked.

"Of course not," said Kenneth. "I'd do it again. If only Tim had been reasonable, or even a little grateful, but 'thank you' just wasn't in that man's vocabulary."

"Who cares if he never thanked you," Shelby said, grabbing his wrists. "It doesn't matter now. Think of the future. Now you can divorce Deirdre. We can have a life. Together."

Now, *this* is interesting, I thought.

"Don't be stupid, Shelby. The police know I had a motive. Deirdre saw to that. She told that lieutenant everything. Who do you think they're going to arrest, if it comes to that?"

"Don't worry, darling —"

Kenneth pulled his hands free of her grasp. "Stop it, Shelby!" Kenneth cried. "What's done is done. It's over now. All of it."

Shelby stared at him in silence for a moment. I waited to hear what would come next, but a mechanical roar drowned out her words. A large truck, its driver most likely lost, thundered around the corner and down Cranberry — and I was standing in the street.

For a moment, I froze like the proverbial trapped deer as the glare of headlights bore down. I blindly leaped, falling into a shadowy stairwell just under the fire escape of Lew's Plumbing and Heating Contractors, Inc.

I had successfully avoided being flattened by the truck *or* detected by my marks — unfortunately, I'd also landed face first in a puddle of water. Spitting in disgust, I rose to my knees, crawled up the steps, and peeked above the edge of the stairwell. But the rain-swept sidewalk under the streetlight was now deserted. Kenneth and Shelby were gone.

Chapter 15

An Open Book

These are not books, lumps of lifeless paper, but minds alive on the shelves . . . far distant in time . . . speaking to us, mind to mind, heart to heart.

— Gilbert Highet

After I returned to the bookstore, I locked the door behind me, shut down the lights, and went straight to the second-floor bathroom to clean up and dry off.

Several times, I tried addressing Jack to discuss what I'd overheard between Shelby and Kenneth, but he wasn't there — or wasn't answering. So I kissed my sleeping Spencer and went to bed.

For a good fifteen minutes, I lay uncomfortably stiff in the dark, wondering vaguely if my ghost had any interest in me — in this particular position. But I assumed he didn't. Or else he'd chosen to honor my request that he not haunt the second floor — or else he *was* here and had clammed up for fear of the grief I'd give him.

Such were my thoughts as I tossed and

turned. Finally I gave up, reached to click on the bedside gooseneck, and grabbed *Shield of Justice* off my nightstand.

To my surprise, even though my eyes were burning from fatigue, I couldn't put the book down. Page after page went by with exhilarating ease.

Brainert had told me he thought the last three books, and especially this one, represented a marked improvement on the older entries in the series, and I had to agree.

Whatever his faults as a human being, Timothy Brennan had, in his waning years, revived his skills as a writer. The story structure of *Shield of Justice* was more sophisticated than in novels past. The expected hard-boiled patois was there, but the speech patterns that had once felt dated and at times corny were now portrayed with a kind of bravado — a false front erected by the world-weary characters to hide their damaged souls. More like the Shamus Award–winning Dennis Lehane than the retro purple prose of Mickey Spillane. In fact, the overall use of language was more refined — adjectives in particular were restrained. And the characters felt richer, deeper.

As one critic had recently put it, where the first sixteen entries in the *Shield* series felt canned and stale, like warmed-over leftovers from tales already told, these latest offerings felt fresh, like the first time Brennan ever put ink to paper:

"Close the door, doll," barked a gruff voice. *"You're ventilating the room . . ."*

I rubbed my eyes. It was nearly 2:00 a.m., and I had promised Aunt Sadie I would be up for church.

"One more chapter," I told myself, even as I yawned and my eyes half-closed. Readers of these books had their favorite parts, and I had just reached mine. The ingenue had entered the story — and the lady was about to enter the lair of Jack Shepard, er, Shield. . . .

"Close the door, doll," barked a gruff voice. *"You're ventilating the room . . ."*

I wanted to read more. I really did. But about then, my eyelids closed completely, and my limbs went limp. . . .

I opened my eyes. Startled, I looked around.

I was no longer lying in bed. I was standing in the doorway of an office — a cluttered and dingy office, with a battered, ink-stained wooden desk and scratched, fading file cabinets. An old typewriter with large, round keys and the word "Underwood" branded across the front sat in the middle of that desk.

I turned to leave. Behind me I saw a narrow hallway with a stained marble floor and fading industrial green paint on the walls. At the far end of that hall an elevator

with heavy glass doors and black iron trim-
mings closed its doors. With a clang, the car
began to descend.

One other office door stood open. A fat
man in suspenders, leaning against the
frame, picked his teeth and stared suspiciously at me.

I turned back toward the office I'd been
facing and stepped inside.

The box was tiny and hot, despite the
black table fan spinning on the window
ledge. Street sounds were muted and far
away. In the middle of the room, a gum-
chewing brunette wearing a jacket with
padded shoulders tapped the keys of the
ancient typewriter on her battered desk. Her
hair looked odd — and I realized she was
wearing her bangs in a roll, like actresses
I'd seen in movies shot in the forties.

A naked lightbulb dangled from the
ceiling, but it wasn't on, since the sun was
shining brightly. Through the half-open
window and the yellowing venetian blinds, I
spotted a rust-encrusted wrought-iron fire
escape. Beyond that, I saw the Manhattan
skyline — but it wasn't quite right. Although
the Empire State Building stood clearly vis-
ible in the distance, its Art Deco facade
dwarfed every other building around it. This
wasn't the New York I remembered; it was
an older city, a city long gone.

A drawer slammed in the next room, and

I jumped. A masculine arm encased in a gunmetal gray sleeve had sent a violent shudder through a heavy file cabinet. The arm waved me over. I hesitated.

"You want to talk, don't you?" said a masculine voice. "Move those gams, then."

I stepped forward, into the man's private office. Once inside, the arm reached out and shoved the door closed. "Let's not make it too easy for the chump in the next office to listen in. Let the bum mind his own business."

The man's voice was deep but not smooth, and there was not a trace of lightness to the monotone. The voice, at least, was familiar to me. I turned and stared up into the iron-jawed grimace of Jack Shepard.

His features appeared chiseled out of unmeltable ice. A flat, square chin held the slash of a one-inch, dagger-shaped scar. Granite-colored eyes stared with unnerving intensity, while shadows beneath suggested a long night — of work or play, I couldn't guess. The gunmetal gray suit was typical forties double-breasted fashion. It flattened his physique, but I wasn't about to believe his shoulders were so ridiculously broad, his waist so trim and narrow.

The overall impression was one of confident virility. He did not appear cheerful in the least, yet there was nothing weak or neurotic or depressive about him. His eyes, his posture, the very energy around him radiated vigor, vitality — life.

A firm hand touched my back, very firm. And rather brazen, I thought with mild irritation. The fingers were boldly splayed, sending heat through my clothing and into my skin. Jack pressed me toward a wooden chair across from the battered desk.

"Take a load off," he said, finally removing the brazen hand. With it went the heat.

I sat down — then yelped. I lifted my leg, wondering what in the world I'd sat on. The quick motion threw up my skirt, which was considerably longer than the skirts I was used to wearing. The material was deep red and of high quality — inside, it was lined with crimson silk. To my surprise, under the lush material my legs were encased in dark nylon stockings. On my feet I saw four-inch heels and wondered vaguely how I had managed to cross the room. The stab of pain, I discovered, was the result of sitting on a twisted metal garter — something I had never worn in my life!

As I hastily adjusted my silky lingerie, I couldn't help but reveal my naked thighs. When I looked up again, Jack Shepard was staring at me, his expression so open and raw, it gave me a moment's shock. The man hadn't bothered in the least to mask his interest. Clearly, he had no sense of propriety.

"Thanks, baby," he said as he unbuttoned his jacket, holding my gaze. "A flash of gam always brightens a Joe's afternoon."

He shrugged out of his jacket and hung it on the back of his chair, a worn leather office antique — at least to my eyes. His white cotton shirt outlined a solid physique. Belying my earlier opinion about the fraud of the double-breasted jacket, the shoulders revealed actually were ridiculously broad; the waist, in truth, trim and narrow; and the dark shoulder holster, strapped tightly against his form, made the muscles even more impossible to miss.

I wouldn't have expected such a slab of man to move around the room with grace. But he circled the heavy desk with the ease of a predator, his gaze continuously summing me up.

Finally he stopped directly in front of my chair and leaned against the block of battered wood behind him. A five o'clock shadow, a shade darker than his sandy-brown hair, dusted his square jaw. His tie was blue and frayed at the tips. I followed his hand as it reached down and lifted a spotted shot glass.

"Fill her up?" he asked, tapping the glass with one finger.

"Pardon me?"

"Would you like a drink? Scotch is all the hooch this bar is serving."

"Scotch will be fine," I replied, surprising myself.

A moment later, Jack placed a glass of amber liquid in my hand.

Jack poured another drink and swirled the glass. Then he leaned against the desk again. An eyebrow rose expectantly.

Stalling for time, I took a sip. The alcohol burned my throat.

"You ready to spill?" he asked while I sputtered.

I nodded, feeling like a suspect under the lamps.

"Tell me what they said. The marks I had you tail."

"It was hard to hear everything. A lot of the words were muffled. But I overheard enough to make me certain they're having an affair."

"Tell me something I don't know. That much was obvious from the way they treated each other in your store. I know feuding lovers when I see them — or ex-lovers."

"Okay, here's something you don't know. I'm pretty sure I heard Kenneth Franken confess to killing Timothy Brennan."

"Oh, you did? Did you? And you actually heard the words 'I killed Brennan' come out of the guy's mouth?"

"Well, no. Not exactly." I shifted uneasily. The long skirt annoyed me, so I pulled it up and crossed my legs. Jack's gaze shifted from my face down to my knees, then slowly up again.

"Well, what 'exactly' did you hear?"

"Shelby asked Ken if he was sorry he did it. Ken said he wasn't and that he'd do it again. And finally Shelby said it was all over and done with anyway — and now Ken could divorce Deirdre and have a life with her."

"Uh-huh."

"So you see, it sure sounds like Ken was the one who might have killed Brennan. He didn't say how or anything, but you seem to think that syringe played a role. Maybe he stuck Brennan with poison somehow."

"Don't you think Brennan would have noticed something like a needle going into him?"

"Oh, right . . . maybe Ken simply pretended that he'd accidentally poked Brennan with a pair of scissors or a sharp pencil. Then maybe he gave the syringe to Shelby, who hid it in the women's room for him — and Shelby had Josh retrieve it."

"Except Josh had to search the women's room, didn't he? If he'd been sent to retrieve it, wouldn't he know where it was?"

"Oh, yes, that's right."

"And what's Kenneth's motive for killing Brennan? What does he gain?"

"I don't know. He didn't like Brennan,

though. He called him a bastard. Maybe he just disliked him enough to kill him."

"Doesn't fit. The man has too much to lose to risk a murder rap when he could have just told the old jerk to go to hell."

I slumped in my seat. "I guess I don't know what to make of it all, then."

Jack's eyes studied me some more. I put my hand to my throat, partially to hide my deep cleavage, where his gaze had decided to settle.

"Eavesdropping's a funny thing, doll, your marks talking about washing the green and you think he's talking about laundering money, when all along he's making a salad."

"Excuse me?"

"Did you hear anything else? Think, now."

"Kenneth said something about how 'thank you' just wasn't in Timothy Brennan's vocabulary. And that Brennan 'stood in the way.'"

"The way of what?" asked Jack.

"I don't know. He didn't say."

"What do you think he meant, then?"

"How should I know?"

Jack narrowed his eyes and finished off his drink in a single gulp. "You've got to listen to more than words in this business, doll. You've got to listen to what's under them."

"I don't know what you mean."

"Ken was bitter because Tim had been

ungrateful for something Ken did for him,"
said Jack. "That means Ken did something
big for Tim — so big that he was still
boiling about it, even with the old man
lying on an M.E.'s slab. Think. What could
Ken have done for Brennan that was so big,
so important that it would still be sticking
in his craw?"

"I don't know. I really don't."

Jack got up from the desk and strode to
the window, his back to me. "To hell with
you. You're not even trying."

"I am so! I tailed them, didn't I? I almost
got run down by a truck, for heaven's sake!"

Jack wheeled. "Then you weren't paying
attention. And that's your problem, doll face,
you want to stick your head in the ground,
avoid confrontation, run and hide from any
jerk who challenges you. You want to keep
thinking the world is some play-fair
sandbox. But you'd better open your eyes,
sweetheart, or next time that truck's going
to leave tread marks on your face. Then
where will that little tyke of yours be — left
without a mother or a father?!"

His words came so fast and furious that I
broke down. Tears rolled over my cheeks. I
lifted my hand to brush them away and noticed the deep red nail enamel on the tips
of my perfectly manicured fingers — a color
I'd never worn in my life. More lost and
confused, my sobbing intensified.

"Turn off the faucet, doll," Jack said gently, coming to my side. "I hate it when dames cry."

My sobs lessened. "That's better," he said. "I only wanted to wise you up. Toughen your hide. You're a sitting duck otherwise, and I'd hate to think . . ."

"What?" I said with a sniffle.

"I don't know . . . I'd hate to think of someone serving you up with orange sauce."

I laughed. A spotless handkerchief was stuffed into my palm, and I swiped at my eyes, leaving streaks of black mascara on the fresh white cloth.

"I'll be happy to stay on the case," he said. "My fee is —"

"I know," I replied, "twenty bucks a day, plus expenses."

There was a long silence. Jack's single finger lifted my chin. I stared into his slate-gray eyes, swallowed hard. I felt his hand caress my cheek, his body lean toward me . . . but I'm a married woman, I thought . . . I can't do this. . . .

I may have felt frozen, torn. But Jack didn't. His rough hands gripped my upper arms and lifted me, pulling my lips to his without the slightest hesitation. My mind went blank. There were no thoughts left. Just feeling. Just his hardness and my softness, the vivid sensual impression of his body . . . the sweet weight of it . . . as it pressed into mine. . . .

"Pen? Penelope, dear! Time for church!"
My eyes slowly opened.
The dream was over. I was in bed, the heaviness of Brennan's open book pressing against my chest.
"Did you hear me, dear?!" called my aunt from the hallway. "Coffee's on. Rise and shine!"

Chapter 16

Revelations

This pool of fire is the second death.
  — Book of Revelation, chapter 20

The late morning sun nearly blinded me as I emerged from the gloomy interior of the First Presbyterian Church of Quindicott. Aunt Sadie's conversation with Gertie Butler — concerning the upcoming church bazaar — didn't look as though it would be ending anytime soon, so I was grateful when Fiona Finch rushed up to me at the top of the flagstone steps, where the wind was whipping strands of my copper hair into one big tangle.

"I have to show you something — at the inn," Fiona whispered, one hand on her blue hat, its wide brim fluttering and flapping.

A small, brown-haired sixty year old, Fiona was the sort of wrenlike person one might easily overlook, except for her piercing dark eyes and flamboyant bird pins. Today's was a black-capped chickadee, floating in the ruffles of her sky-blue blouse. She had at least two hundred of these molded feathered friends, and once a week she dragged her husband, Barney, around to every yard sale within miles on her never-ending quest for more.

Although few would ever guess it, Fiona was also an avid true crime enthusiast, her most recent purchase from our store being an out-of-print hardcover edition of James Reston Jr.'s *Our Father Who Art in Hell*, the story of how Jim Jones led one thousand members of his People's Temple cult into killing themselves with poison-laced Kool-Aid.

Along with her husband, Fiona ran the town's only hotel — many believed for the sole purpose of listening in on her guests' private conversations. And with Deirdre, Kenneth, Shelby, and Josh all staying at Finch's Inn, I was pretty sure Fiona had some dirt to dish.

I had an hour to spare before the book-store opened and I was more than a little cu-rious. So when Fiona approached, of course I touched Aunt Sadie's arm and said, "Something's up. I'm going with Fiona."

"Not without me, you're not," Sadie re-plied, and we took off.

I breathed a sigh of relief as I steered my aunt quickly past young Rev. Waterman. I didn't know what Sadie might have said to him, if given the chance, but I doubted it would have been charitable.

During today's service the reverend had

made a general announcement after his sermon: "The church parking lot is *not* to be used as a solution to the business district's parking problems. Given that this terrible problem was started by an unfortunate event at one of the town's businesses, I'd appreciate the owners of that particular business seeing to it that the cars of their customers stay *out* of the church lot."

Rev. Waterman's ice-blue eyes were staring directly at me and Sadie while he delivered his postsermon sermon. Other members of the congregation nervously peeked in our direction — with the exception of the Knitters for Charity Club, who openly glared — just to make sure we got the message.

Loud and clear, ladies!

(Apparently the Knitters had arrived at the church for their Saturday afternoon meeting to find the lot completely full. They were ready to kill — and a dozen pissed-off Presbyterian matrons armed with knitting needles can be as dangerous as your average weapon of mass destruction.)

By the time the service ended, I wanted to run for cover. Sadie, of course, was loaded for bear. Naturally, I was grateful to Fiona Finch for the distraction.

Despite my earlier misgivings, I was glad Spencer wasn't with us today. Before I left for church, he was chauffeured to his cousin's birthday party in Newport.

I knew from past experience that such an event would include a catered lunch; a series of children's games organized and run by the McClure nannies; a hired magician; live music; a rented carousel; hot air balloon rides; three flavors of cake; and, once twilight descended, twenty minutes of fireworks that culminated in the birthday boy's name written in lights across the sky.

I frankly wasn't thrilled about Spencer going anywhere near his father's family, but he wanted to go, and I really did feel guilty saying no. I still didn't like the McClures. And I didn't trust them. But they were Spencer's relatives, and he had a right to see his cousins and spend a day playing with children his own age.

The weather was glorious, too. Except for the whistling wind, all evidence of last night's storm was gone. The sun felt warm and pleasant as we strolled along Cranberry Street. Families and couples were drifting toward the common, already taking up benches for the free concert this afternoon in the band shell.

I'd heard some honking in the direction of the empty old Embry lot. The reason why would be apparent within the hour, but at that moment I was walking swiftly in the other direction, and my mind was elsewhere.

"What's going on?" I asked Fiona.

Fiona shushed me. "Not yet," she said with

a hiss, her eyes darting suspiciously. "The wrong people might overhear us."

So we continued our journey in silence until we heard a man calling: "Stop! Wait!"

We turned to find our fortysomething mailman, Seymour Tarnish, running toward us, gesturing wildly. By the time he got to our side, Seymour could hardly speak.

"I . . . was looking . . . for you." His round face was flushed and covered with a sheen of perspiration. Bending at his thick waist, he leaned on his knees, gasping for air.

I was more than a little intrigued to discover what had gotten slow-moving Seymour excited enough to gallop like Seabiscuit down Cranberry Street.

"Simmer down, Seymour," Aunt Sadie insisted. "You look like you're having a heart attack."

"We have to . . . get to . . . a television," Seymour wheezed between gulps of air. "Pronto!"

"What's this about?" Fiona demanded. She displayed little patience for Seymour's antics — especially when they threatened to steal her own gossipy thunder.

"Rather not try . . . to explain," Seymour replied, mopping the sweat from his receding hairline with the sleeve of his flannel shirt, "you . . . have to see for yourselves."

"We can use the television in the common room," Fiona said.

"Can you make it, Seymour?" Aunt Sadie asked.

"I'm fine," Seymour said between gasps.

Situated at the end of a drive lined with hundred-year-old weeping willows, Finch's Inn was a classic Queen Anne–style Victorian era mansion. And, as Fiona liked to point out, the Queen Anne style itself made its debut just next door, in Newport (the William Watts Sherman House circa 1874).

Four floors of rooms boasted breathtaking views of Quindicott Pond, a good-sized body of salt water fed by a narrow, streamlike inlet that raced in and out with the tides from the Atlantic shoreline miles away.

A nature trail, one of the favorites of birders in the region, circled the pond and stretched into the backwoods, following the inlet for about eight miles. The inn rented bicycles for the trail and rowboats for the pond, which was usually pretty well stocked with fish.

Although Fiona and her husband, Barney, had not yet found the resources to fulfill their dream of opening a gourmet restaurant, they ran a respectable inn with thirteen guest rooms, all boasting fireplaces and decorated with their own unique character.

The four of us climbed the six long steps and thundered across the wide, wraparound wooden porch, which sat upon a sturdy gray fieldstone foundation. Fiona and Barney had even repainted the place in its original, dark, rich, high Victorian colors: reddish-brown on the clapboards of the main body, and a combination of olive green and old gold on the moldings and the spindlelike ornaments that served as a porch railing.

Brick chimneys, bay windows, steep shingle-covered gables, and a corner turret completed the picture — and a pretty picture it was. I just loved the place.

"You know how to find the common room," Fiona said as we walked through the stained-glass front door, the grand oak staircase greeting us like a solemn butler. "I'll fetch the things I wanted to show you," she tossed to me.

As Fiona headed for the carved mahogany reception desk just off the entryway, Sadie and Seymour rushed along the hall and into the great parlor, which occupied most of the left side of the mansion. I followed more leisurely, soaking up the turn-of-the-century touches: the striped gold wallpaper, dark wood moldings, and the required Victorian clutter, from colorful vases and dried flowers to various glass-fronted collector's cabinets of tiny porcelain birds.

Then I came upon the portraits. Two large rectangular renderings in dark wood frames, surrounded by five oval-shaped gilt-edged miniatures. All of the oil paintings depicted the same woman — the enigmatic "Harriet," the Finch Inn's version of Beatrice, the solitary painter who'd occupied Newport's Cliffside Inn at the turn of the century and left a thousand self-portraits upon her death.

Harriet McClure didn't leave nearly so many paintings, more like a hundred, but it had, nevertheless, disturbed the McClure relatives enough to sell her mansion to the Finch family — though the McClures kept ownership of most of the grounds, along with their holdings in town and around the pond.

I'd never heard the whole story about Harriet. I just knew she'd lived alone for years, save for the housekeeper and caretaker, Barney Finch's grandmother and grandfather. She was occasionally seen taking lone strolls around the pond, but other than that, she seldom mixed with any townsfolk.

Upon her mysterious death at age forty-five, a hundred self-portraits were found among her things in the upstairs rooms. The Finches hung a dozen throughout the house — the best of the lot, so the story goes. The rest they'd tossed onto the fire during a particularly hard winter.

"The pool of fire . . ." I murmured, suddenly remembering Rev. Waterman's sermon.

I saw the dead, the great and the lowly, standing before the throne, and the scrolls were opened. Then another scroll was opened, the book of life. The dead were judged according to their deeds. . . . Anyone whose name was not found written in the book of life was thrown into the pool of fire. . . .

As I stared at poor, dead Harriet's brown eyes and upswept hair, her high white Victorian collar encircling her throat, I felt a shiver go through me — not unlike the shivers I'd felt in the bookstore — and I began to wonder. . . .

Given my strange experiences with the ghost of Jack Shepard, could there be more spirits hanging around Quindicott? And if there were, what were they hanging around *for?*

"The pool of fire is the second death," I murmured. "The *second* death." I stared hard at the portrait. I felt a little shiver go through me once more, but I heard no voice, saw no vision . . . and so I joined the others.

None of the inn guests were in the great parlor when I got there, which wasn't a surprise on such a beautiful day. I sat on the smooth floral upholstery of the carved rosewood and mahogany sofa, admiring the gilded ballroom mirror above the large fireplace and the bay window, where streaming sunlight washed the hanging baskets of flowers.

Seymour, meanwhile, banged open the large armoire, meant to tastefully hide the entertainment system. Remote in hand, his thumb began to bounce up and down on the buttons faster than I thought a human digit could move. Images flew across the screen like a wildly spinning roll in a slot machine. Finally the images slowed and landed on a grinning woman holding a box of plastic food storage bags.

"That's the jackpot?" I teased Seymour. "You want us to switch brands of Baggies?"

"CNN Headline News has the heaviest rotation," he explained. "Maybe after these commercials."

Sadie and I watched an ad for Caribbean cruises, and another for a phone service plan. Seymour pulled up a cane-backed chair, facing us, not the television.

"I want to see the look on your faces!" he said.

Fiona breezed into the room with a tray of ice tea. Under her arm was a bundle of papers.

"Here you are," she said as she put the papers on the coffee table. Then she handed everyone a tall glass of homemade ice tea with a sprig of mint in it. Fiona glanced at the commercials and put her hands on her hips. Scowling, she faced Seymour.

"Now, what is this all about?"

"Here it is!" Seymour cried, sloshing ice tea as he pointed to the television screen.

I found myself watching a videotape of a crowded room, the audience members packed into row after row of padded folding chairs, all facing a carved wooden podium.

"Good lord, that's our store!" Sadie cried.

"Oh, no," I murmured, guessing what was coming next. "Oh, no . . ."

There he was, big, florid Timothy Brennan interrupting his lecture to take a long swig of bottled water — just seconds after I stepped into camera range and handed it to him. A deft edit, and the screen revealed Brennan choking, then collapsing. The announcer's solemn voice summed up Brennan's long career as the visuals switched to a black-and-white clip of the old Jack Shield television show, then the cover of *Shield of Justice*.

"It had to be those two dudes doing the camera work," Seymour said. "They were probably freelancers, and they didn't strike me as all that sharp. I bet some agent approached them, brokered a deal for the networks."

"Howie Westwood," I murmured, suddenly feeling nauseated.

"Who?" asked Seymour.

"A man came to the store yesterday posing as a reporter for *Independent Bookseller* magazine. He wasn't."

"He wasn't?" asked Sadie. "How do you know?"

"I know," I said. "Because everything about him was fake." As Jack Shepard's ghost pointed out, of course, but I didn't want to believe him at the time.

"But that doesn't prove anything," said Sadie.

"Believe me, he was the agent," I said. "His eyes lit up like July Fourth fireworks when I mentioned the event had been taped."

"He must have made a killing," said Seymour. "Considering the tape's news value."

"What news value?" Sadie asked, outraged. "Authors are like everyone else. They keel over and die every day."

"That's not why they're playing it. Listen!" Seymour pointed at the television.

On the screen, the image of Timothy Brennan's final moments were replayed, but this time a tinted circle highlighted the water bottle in Brennan's hand.

". . . Authorities will neither confirm nor deny that foul play is suspected in the death of this best-selling mystery author," the announcer said. "Though no suspects have been identified, CNN *has* learned that the Rhode Island State Police crime lab has conducted a toxicology study on the contents of the bottle, which the local police impounded the night of Brennan's death.

"An anonymous source tells us there is evidence the bottle had been tampered with. Meanwhile, first-edition copies of *Shield of Justice* with the unique stamp authenticating its purchase at the bookstore where Brennan died are now going for as high as $300 a piece on eBay. In other news . . . ."

"It's on *every* channel," Seymour crowed. "I saw it this morning and came to warn you."

My shoulders slumped, and I held my head. Yesterday had been bad enough. If every news channel was carrying this story, then who knew what was coming next? Sure, I wanted Buy the Book to be profitable, but praying for rain doesn't mean you welcome a hurricane!

"The police suspect murder," Sadie murmured, her face pale.

Well, I *had* tried to warn her, but Sadie had chosen to ignore the signs. I reached out and took her hand. With the other, Sadie lifted her glass and swallowed some ice tea, all the while staring at the television screen.

My own reaction could best be described as muted. Given my conversation with Jack, the syringenapping by Josh, and the conversation I'd overheard when I'd eavesdropped on Shelby and Kenneth, I wasn't all that surprised at this development. The hidden syringe had obviously played a part in corrupting the water bottle. But *what* had been in that syringe?

"What did they mean, 'the bottle was tampered with'?" Sadie asked.

"Poison!" Fiona Finch said, her cheeks rosy with exhilaration. "I'll just bet the cops found traces of deadly poison in that water bottle."

"The problem is, I don't see how that's possible," I said. "I randomly selected the bottle myself from over a dozen set aside especially for Brennan."

"Did you set them aside?" asked Seymour.

"No. It was Linda Cooper-Logan who told me they'd been set aside. She started helping me with the refreshments after some of the guests started swarming the table."

"You're not suggesting Linda murdered Brennan," said Seymour.

"Of course not! None of this makes any sense. How could the killer have known which bottle I'd grab of the dozen? And if they were all poisoned, then why didn't anyone else get sick and die? After Eddie and his partner arrived that night, they took the bottle I'd given to Brennan as evidence, but that's all they impounded. We were all cooped up in the store for hours giving statements, and there were plenty of people who ended up drinking from those reserved bottles of Brennan's — even me. And, like I said, none of us got sick or died."

"You know, Pen . . . that's pretty incriminating," said Seymour, lines furrowing his forehead.

"What's 'pretty incriminating'?"

"Well . . . you said it yourself: *You* were the one who handed the bottle to Brennan — which would be opportunity. And your store is profiting from his death — which would be motive."

"I know, I know. I've thought of that already," I said.

But Sadie wouldn't hear of it. "Don't be ridiculous, Seymour! Penelope is not responsible for *anyone's* death!"

An image suddenly came over me: my hand on the polished knob, the door swinging open, my late husband's pinstriped pajamas, arms raised like wings on the fourteenth-floor ledge. I winced.

"Sadie, calm down," said Seymour. "Pen didn't kill Brennan. I know that. I'm just saying it doesn't look good. That's all. And I just think Pen should be ready for the State Police to question her again."

"Well," Fiona said with a self-satisfied smirk, "I don't know how one bottle could have been tainted and not the others. But I do know one thing . . ." Fiona tapped the papers on the coffee table.

"If it *is* murder, then *I've* solved the crime!"

Sadie and I gaped at Fiona. Seymour slammed down his ice tea, sloshing liquid onto the coffee table — much to Fiona's annoyance. She snatched up the papers before they were saturated.

"Are we ready to pay attention now?" Fiona asked. We all nodded like schoolchildren.

"On the night of Timothy Brennan's death,

Mr. and Mrs. Franken returned to the inn and had a huge argument. Why, they were so loud you couldn't help but hear every word."

"And if you *couldn't* hear every word you could always place an empty glass against the wall," Seymour quipped.

"Was it Mr. Franken doing the arguing?" I asked.

"No," Fiona replied, glaring at Seymour. "It was *Mrs.* Franken. She was screaming about some woman."

"Ah," said Seymour. *"Entrée la femme."*

"Huh?" said Sadie.

"Enter the woman," Fiona translated.

"How do you know it was a woman?" Seymour asked.

Sadie and I nodded. Good question.

"I heard her *name*," Fiona replied, not a little indignant that her eavesdropping skills were being questioned. "It was *Anna*."

"Anna? Are you sure?" I asked, surprised. I'd expected her to say "Shelby."

But Fiona seemed certain. "Mrs. Franken kept repeating that she knew all about this Anna, and how dangerous this Anna was."

"Obviously Mrs. Franken suspected foul play," said Seymour, scratching the back of his neck.

"Darn right," Fiona replied. "Mrs. Franken kept repeating that this Anna person killed her father. But I also got the distinct impression that she thought her husband was somehow involved in her father's death, too. They argued for a while, then things got very quiet. When I made up their room in the morning, I discovered that Mr. Franken had spent the night on the love seat."

"Anna *Worth*," I murmured.

"Who?" asked Seymour.

"Oh, Anna Worth!" cried Sadie. "Of course! She was there in our store the night Brennan died."

"And she is?" asked Seymour.

"The cereal heiress," said Sadie. "Worth Flakes and Nuts. She's the one got herself in all that trouble for shooting her bodyguard's gun at her boyfriend in front of that New York nightclub."

"Why, Sadie Thornton," said Fiona, "I'm impressed that you remembered that whole Anna Worth scandal!"

"Of course," said Sadie with a wave of her hand.

"Okay," said Seymour, "so she was there the night Brennan was killed. That doesn't mean she killed him."

"Yes," I agreed. "Despite what you overheard about some 'Anna,' *if* Brennan was murdered by Anna *Worth*, we need a motive. Can you connect the dots between Anna Worth and Timothy Brennan?" *Connect the dots*, I repeated silently to myself — if only Jack could hear me now!

"There's no connection," said Seymour.

"I'll bet Anna Worth didn't even *know* Timothy Brennan."

"You'd lose that bet, mailman," said Fiona. "Look!"

Fiona thrust the pages from the top of the pile into my hand — microfiche copies from archived magazine pages. The ads and the styles of clothing indicated that these clippings were nearly twenty years old. Sadie leaned forward and studied the pages. Seymour read them over my shoulder.

"Where did you get this stuff?" I asked.

"First I spent a few hours on the Internet," Fiona replied. "Then I called Robby Tucker to let me into the library early this morning."

Fiona smiled again, as smugly as before. "These clippings clearly establish a connection between Brennan and Anna Worth — and Anna Worth's motive for murder," she declared.

"Maybe you better explain this to us rubes?" Seymour said somewhat skeptically.

Fiona glanced over her shoulder to make sure no one was lurking about. Not satisfied that we were alone, she bit her lip, rose, went to the heavy parlor doors, and slid them shut. She returned, but when she spoke again, it was a whisper.

"It was *Gossip* magazine that kept Anna Worth in the public eye for months after the nightclub shooting two decades ago," Fiona continued. "If you look at those articles, you

220

will see that every single story about the heiress and her troubles had the same byline. All of them were written by Timothy Brennan."

"That's *right!*" Seymour said, snapping his fingers. "Brennan was a New York reporter, and he kept writing for magazines, even after the Shield series was published. That's in his bio."

Fiona showed us a three-page story with photos of Anna Worth, clad in disco finery, partying with several well-known celebrities from that hedonistic era in New York City social history.

"According to the first story, published less than a week after the scandal, Brennan claims he actually witnessed the shooting while on a date at the nightclub where it occurred."

Fiona faced me. "Obviously Brennan sold his exclusive tale to *Gossip* magazine. So he'd single-handedly made this relatively minor incident a national story — to the point where Johnny Carson was making jokes about Anna Worth on the *Tonight Show*.

"The public obviously loved reading about her, so the magazine hired Brennan to file ongoing reports about Anna Worth. Brennan gathered statements from victims and witnesses that contradicted Anna Worth's version of the events, which tainted her defense at the trial.

"In the weeks and months after, Brennan published stories about Anna Worth's past. About her friends. About her father's efforts to get his daughter cleared . . ."

As she spoke, Fiona turned page after page. Each one featured a photo of Anna Worth — and the byline Timothy Brennan.

"Anna's father hired high-priced lawyers. Then he tried to pay off the injured bystanders, and he'd even botched an attempt to bribe a New York City judge — which led to charges against him, too.

"And Brennan was on it every step of the way. Of course, by that time there were plenty of other journalists involved, not unlike the O.J. case, but it was actually Brennan who'd started it all, because he'd been an eyewitness. He was even the one who'd first labeled Anna as 'the most dangerous party girl in Manhattan.' "

As Fiona spoke, I leafed through the photocopies. I did remember the scandal, but not all these details — and certainly not the fact that Brennan had been the one to start the ball rolling.

"Later articles show that Brennan continued reminding the public of Anna well after the incident," continued Fiona. "He was right there with a photographer to record her release from jail. And in a more recent piece — in a special edition *Gossip* magazine titled 'Where Are They Now?' — Brennan updated the public on Anna's subsequent brushes with the law, including bizarre incidents of shoplifting, as well as her repeated attempts to kick her cocaine habit."

Fiona sighed. "If it *was* murder, there's the motive."

I had to agree. "It looks like Brennan deliberately set out to ruin Anna Worth's life."

"Well, the woman did have a little something to do with that herself," Aunt Sadie replied.

"Nevertheless," said Fiona, "you can see why Anna Worth would carry a grudge."

"But did she hate Timothy Brennan enough to poison him?" Seymour asked. "And how the heck did she manage to poison him and no one else?"

Fiona shrugged. "I don't know how she did it. But if Brennan made my every mistake public, I'd have killed him myself."

"Remind me never to get on your bad side," said Seymour. He was about to drink from the glass in his hand, but set it down instead.

I raised an eyebrow. "Don't worry, Seymour, I didn't touch your glass."

Seymour stared at me a moment; then he burst out laughing.

Aunt Sadie and Fiona Finch laughed, too. So did I. It felt good — a wonderful release of tension.

And then I swear I heard a fourth woman

laughing in the room, right there with us. With a little shiver, I remembered the twelve portraits of Harriet still hanging in the place.

"Aunt Sadie," I said quickly, "let's get back to our store."

Chapter 17

A Worthy Suspect

O. Henry wrote of crime, but he seldom wasted precious words on the dry-as-dust business of questioning stupid witnesses and hunting — through endless pages — for clues that mean little or nothing when found. . . . He wrote about real people — and the reader suffered and rejoiced with them, in direct proportion with their reality. . . .
— Opening statement by "The Editor," *Detective Tales*, August 1935

"Excuse me, lady, but you're cutting the line."

"Excuse *me*," Aunt Sadie shot back, "but I'm trying to open my store!"

Cameras clicked and lightbulbs flashed. A microphone emblazoned with the letters of a local television station was thrust into Sadie's face.

"Who do you think committed the Bookstore Murder?" a pretty young blond demanded. Behind her, a cameraman with a backward baseball cap tried to film us over the heads of the crowd.

"Er . . . ah," Sadie stammered.

"No comment," I said in a clipped tone, channeling every suspicious politician I'd seen accosted by the press for the past decade.

But the reporter wouldn't quit.

"Do you feel it is right to profit from this crime?" she asked, moving the mike from her face to mine so fast I got it on the chin. *Yow!*

"You heard the lady. No comment!" shouted Seymour. As I rubbed the bruised skin, he quickly stepped in front of me. "If you want to get into the store, you have to get in line like everybody else."

I appreciated the fact that Seymour had taken point, but if there *was* an actual line to get into Buy the Book, I couldn't see it. Just about a hundred people milling around, blocking the front of the bookstore and the other business fronts along the block — most of them mercifully closed on a Sunday. There were dozens of cars parked — and double-parked — up and down Cranberry Street, and I saw a few satellite vans as well. More journalists were no doubt lurking about, waiting to spring.

Horns blared as people ignored the bumper-to-bumper traffic and ran across the street in front of moving cars.

"I can't believe this," I said with a moan.

Seymour shook his head. "It's the insidious

power of the mass media."

Seymour, Sadie, and I again tried to push through the crowd, but we might as well have been trying to part the Red Sea. The sidewalk was packed and people were spilling over into the street, sitting on cars, the curb, even in the doorways of other Cranberry Street businesses. Clearly, these folks had been here awhile — the sidewalk was littered with paper cups, crumpled wrappers, and empty bags. I made a mental note to buy a steel trash can and plant it in front of the store — soonest.

Bud Napp, the sixtyish owner of the town's hardware store, cruised by in his truck, which was crawling along with the rest of the traffic. "Someone tore down the chains the city council put up around the Embry lot!" he crowed through his open window, giving a clenched-fist, power-to-the-people, up-with-the-revolution arm gesture. "Now the lot is jammed with parked cars!"

"Pinkie's gonna love *that*," said Aunt Sadie.

The traffic began to move and Bud drove on, whistling tunelessly.

So the news was not *all* bad. Bud was positively ecstatic (he'd been pushing to make that abandoned lot a parking area for as long as anyone could remember), and I spotted a long line of folks waiting to get into Cooper's Bakery for coffee and pastries. There was a long line in front of Koh's Grocery, too. Mr.

Koh, who was restocking fruit on the outdoor stalls, saw Sadie and me trying to negotiate the crowd. Smiling, he bowed to us. I bowed back and he actually beamed!

We got another positive wave from Joe Franzetti, who was throwing pizza dough in his store's window. His booths and tables were full, and the sidewalk was jammed with customers waiting for a slice.

In front of our own store, Sadie impatiently pushed against the crowd again. Like a living thing, the throng pushed back.

"Folks, you can't get into the store if we can't open it," I pleaded.

The mob moved a little, but there were angry cries as people were crowded off the sidewalk. Suddenly I heard the sound of breaking glass as a bottle hit the concrete.

"That's it!" Seymour roared. "What the hell do you people think this is, a mosh pit?!" To my surprise, the crowd drew back as people scrambled to get out of Seymour's way. "Make a hole! Make a hole!" he shouted.

I turned to my aunt. "Make a hole?"

"Navy term," she told me. "He's obviously flashing back to those four years when he was an enlisted man."

"Bite me, asshole!" someone shouted from the crowd.

Seymour whirled to face the heckler, who wore faded Levi's, a St. Francis College sweatshirt, and a red bandanna around his head.

"I'm a *postal worker,* buster!" Seymour cried, a vein bulging on his forehead. "Do you really want a piece of me?!"

The heckler shrunk back in terror. And the mass of people seemed to finally break and flow back like ice on a thawing river. They might not respond to orders very well, but they all understood the meaning of the term "going postal."

"That's more *like* it," cried Seymour. "Now let's form a nice, orderly, single-file line starting right over here. That way everybody will get in to see the pretty store."

While Seymour wrangled the crowd, Sadie unlocked the door and we slipped inside. Seymour came in behind us, but only after he issued a final warning to the college student.

"I'm keeping an eye on you, bub."

Once through the door, I turned to Seymour. "Thanks," I said. "We never would have gotten through that crowd ourselves."

"My pleasure," he said. "I'll stick around if you like. It's Sunday, so I've got no mail to deliver, and my ice cream truck's out of supplies till Monday."

"That would be really great," I said.

"We'll pay you in trade," said Sadie. "First dibs on any pulp magazines that come in for the next six months. And you can have the first two *free.*"

Seymour gave her a thumbs-up.

I jumped behind the counter and booted up the register, the monitor, and the computer. Sadie glanced at her watch.

"Time to open," she announced.

I took a deep breath, then nodded. Sadie turned the sign around to read OPEN and unlocked the front door.

As the crowd rushed in, I saw flashing lights at the curb. Officer Eddie Franzetti came rushing up to the doorway, his hand firmly on the billy club attached to his dark blue uniform's utility belt.

"Pen, you need help here?" he asked. "I would have been here sooner, but Rev. Waterman was crazed about setting up barricades to keep cars out of his church lot."

"No problem, Eddie. Seymour helped us out with the crowd control."

"Seymour? Seymour Tarnish?" Eddie's dark brown eyes widened, the thick eyebrows rising. He lifted the hat off his short black hair and wiped his forehead with the same hand, scratching the back of his head before putting the hat on again.

"Oh, yeah," I said. "Seymour was great. And I'm sorry about the litter on the sidewalk. I'm getting a trash can first thing tomorrow. So let Pinkie — uh, I mean Councilwoman Binder-Smith — know that in case she calls you guys up to complain about us again."

"Aw, that woman complains on a daily basis. About *everyone*. Listen, I better go," Eddie said. "The Embry lot is a mess. Someone ripped the chains down and it's total anarchy." He eyed the crowd warily. "But if there's any more trouble here, you be sure to call me anytime. For *anything*, okay?"

"Thanks, Eddie," I called.

"Save a copy of *Shield of Justice* for me, too," he tossed back.

"Will do! And tell MaryJo and the kids we're getting the next Harry Potter in soon." (So Harry Potter wasn't technically a part of the mystery genre. So what? There *were* mystery elements — and no bookstore owner in her right mind would say no to stocking it.)

I watched Eddie drive off, then started my own thrilling new installment of *Adventures in Retail*.

"I feel a presence in this place. An unearthly presence. A spirit of the dead."

The speaker was a woman who'd been waiting among the throng. She was past middle age, with long, frizzy, gray hair. She stared at me through wide, unblinking green eyes.

"You feel it, too," she said.

Okay, she looked like she'd stepped out of Central Casting, or one of those classic old Universal horror films featuring a band of singing and dancing Gypsies — right down

231

to the long, flowing, multicolored dress and Birkenstocks. But what the hell . . . I was desperate. Maybe this woman *could* sense spiritual beings. Maybe she *was* channeling Jack Shepard. Maybe she had some answers.

Nix on that, dollface.

Jack had spoken inside my head for the first time today. I hated myself for it, but I felt my heartbeat quicken just a little bit.

This battle-ax is one booze jag away from the drunk tank.

"Thanks for the valuable input, Jack," I said silently. "Good morning to you, too."

Seymour, at his post near the front door, pointed to his head and twirled his finger. *Cuckoo!* Then he silently mouthed something that looked like, "CNN really brings out the lunatics, doesn't it?"

"Oh, Seymour," I thought to myself. "If you only knew what I knew."

I turned to the woman and asked, "Can I help you?"

"The spirit is in torment. It cries out!" the woman said, loud enough for the other customers to notice. "The spirit demands justice."

This woman sounds sincere, I decided. My heart began to beat faster, wondering for a moment if Jack could be wrong.

"Is this woman really a sensitive?" I asked Jack.

Yeah, she's sensitive, all right, said Jack. *To*

bathtub gin and rotgut whiskey.

The woman spun on her heels, her dress billowing.

"Oh, yes," she said, gazing at the ceiling. "It is the ghost of Timothy Brennan, cursed to haunt these premises until his murderer is punished."

Brennan? said Jack. *Here for eternity? Look around, toots. There ain't a barstool or bookie in sight. Why would Brennan bother to stay in this place?*

"I must listen for his voice!" she cried.

Shut her up, would you? Jack told me. *Or I'll scare the hell out of her myself.*

"Don't do that!" I silently warned Jack. "There are too many people around!"

"Ma'am," I said, touching her shoulder. She spun on me.

"Do not touch a sensitive!" she screeched. I recoiled.

That's it! Jack cried.

A moment later, the woman's eyes bulged. Her jaw dropped.

"What's the matter?" I asked. "Are you all right?"

"J-J-ack . . . J-j-jack Sh-sh-shepard!" she stammered, pointing at me.

"Great," I thought. "Jack, what in the world are you doing?"

I'm projecting, he said. *On you.*

NOW GET THE HELL OUT OF MY STORE!

The woman screamed and ran. No one seemed to be aware of Jack or me. Or the fact that he'd just screamed so loud in my head I'd automatically put my hands to my ears — as useless as that was. All eyes were on the crazed lady running for the door.

"Well, that was certainly an education," I told him.

Ha! Didn't think I had it in me, did you?

"Actually, I didn't."

Well, it's not a piece of cake or anything, said Jack. *But when I'm really worked up . . .*

"Remind me never to really work you up."

With a sigh, my gaze followed the trail of the exiting lady — and my body froze. I felt as though I'd seen a ghost — but not Jack's ghost, more like the ghost of felons past.

As the "sensitive" barreled through the front doorway, she jostled a familiar middle-aged woman. It was Anna Worth, the cereal heiress herself — returning to the scene of the crime, if Fiona Finch's theory was correct.

This time Anna Worth came with a solicitous-looking older man in tow. He looked like a professor, graying at the temples and wearing tweed, with leather patches on his jacket.

Anna Worth, on the other hand, looked the height of fashion. Her sheer peach pantsuit was beautifully tailored, and pink-tinted sunglasses sat on top of her pale blond shoulder-length hair. I probably would not have recognized her had I not seen dozens of photographs of her at various ages not two hours ago. Seymour recognized her, too, and he casually moved toward the counter.

Despite her elegant attire, Anna Worth gave the impression not of a regal heiress but of a mouse stepping into the home of a very hungry feline. The farther into the store she moved, the more noticeably her shoulders drooped, the more rapidly her eyes began to dart about. When they finally strayed in the direction of the community space, she visibly paled.

The older man instantly reacted to her discomfort. He took her arm and steered the now nervous wreck of an heiress to the other end of the store, seating her in one of the Shaker rockers. She sat, and he kneeled at her side, speaking softly into her ear.

"Pssssst, Jack!" I thought as loudly as I could. "Be a help, would you, and eavesdrop on their conversation for me?"

I received no reply, and just hoped he had already gotten the same idea and was preoccupied with his "surveillance work" already.

Seymour leaned against the counter and said in a conversational tone, "Gee, maybe murderers do return to the scene of the crime."

"Shhhhhh!" I hissed.

"Come on, you don't really think this

eighties flashback bumped off Brennan, do you? Fiona Finch has read one too many true crime books."

"Look, look, she's moving again," Sadie whispered from the corner of her mouth.

Anna Worth had risen from the rocker and, with childlike baby steps, she began to move. Her companion followed her, rubbing his chin and eyeing Anna closely. The woman paused, and the man rushed to her side. Whispering, they moved through aisles of books, never once glancing at a title. Whatever they were doing here, they certainly weren't here to purchase some light beach reading.

Seymour grinned and poked my arm. "Here's your chance," he said.

"Huh?"

"Follow them."

"They'll see me."

"But you *own* the place," Seymour insisted. "You're practically help. And rich people like Anna Worth never notice the help. Ever. So go over and restock the shelves."

I must have had a blank expression on my face because Seymour didn't wait for my reply. Rolling his eyes, he reached into my carefully arranged new-releases section and grabbed a handful of titles off the table — the new Patricia Cornwell paperback, a Janet Evanovich, a brand-new thriller by Ed McBain, a short fiction collection by James

Ellroy — and thrust them into my arms.

"Go restock the shelves," he repeated, giving me a push.

Resigning myself to the inevitable, I pushed my black rectangular glasses up my nose; took a deep breath; and, assuming an air of what I hoped was casual indifference, set off to put copies of my brand-new releases among the older titles. A retailing erratum, but I told myself I was doing it in the name of ratiocination.

It didn't take me but a minute to spot Anna Worth and her friend. They were standing near the Dennis Lehane novels. The closest letter I had in my hand was "M," so Ed McBain would have to do. I approached the couple unseen. Fortunately, they were lost in conversation.

"Work through it," the man whispered. "Face your darkest fears or they will own you, Anna."

Anna Worth replied, but so softly I couldn't hear her words.

I moved a little closer, pretending to adjust the Kellerman section — Jonathan and Faye — and even a *Harry* Kellerman rabbi mystery.

"You hated that man," Tweedy replied. "How did it feel to watch him fall . . . to watch him die?"

His words startled me, and the entire Faye Kellerman collection tumbled to the floor.

Anna Worth and the man spun around to face me. Anna had that deer-in-the-headlights stare.

It's now or never, doll, Jack said in my head. *Go ahead and ask.*

Before I knew it, my mouth moved, and I spoke. "You're Anna Worth, aren't you? My name is Penelope Thornton-McClure, the co-owner of this store. I saw you here the other night, when Timothy Brennan died."

Anna's mouth moved, but no words came out. I could see torment — guilt, perhaps? — on her face. Whatever it was, her look made me bolder.

"Why were you here, Ms. Worth?" I said. "Surely you're no fan of Mr. Brennan's work."

Anna Worth clutched Tweedy's arm and turned her face away. "Please, Doctor, do something," she whispered.

"Ms. McClure," the man said indignantly, "surely you can see that this woman is distraught!"

"I can see that," I replied. Then I turned to Anna Worth. "I am terribly sorry if I upset you. Of course, we're all upset, knowing that we may have all witnessed a murder right here in this store the other night. You have heard the news, Ms. Worth? The police suspect foul play . . . poison."

But Anna Worth really didn't react to this news. She just blinked. It was the man in the tweed jacket who did most of the reacting. "I think you've upset my patient quite enough for one day," he said, stepping between us.

"Your *patient?*"

Tweedy adjusted his tie. "My name is Dr. Stuart Nablaum, a practicing psychologist in Newport. Ms. Worth is my patient. I accompanied her two nights ago, and today, because we have some unfinished emotional business with Mr. Brennan."

"You were here with Anna Worth the other night?" I asked.

"Of course," he said. "Every moment. Anna is in such a delicate emotional state right now she can go nowhere without supervision — my supervision. Nor could I be so remiss as to have Ms. Worth face Timothy Brennan alone."

"Why did she want to face Brennan at all?" I asked.

The man's nostrils flared, and I thought he was going to throw me out of my own store. Then Anna spoke.

"Tell her," she said in a breathy, little-girl voice.

"But Anna —"

"Please tell her, Stuart."

Dr. Nablaum scowled at me. "Not that it's any of your business, but Anna came here to face Timothy Brennan and tell him how much he had hurt her."

"The scandal, you mean?" I said. "The articles Brennan wrote about it?"

Dr. Nablaum frowned. "Mrs. McClure, you probably don't understand how hard a person has to fight to overcome an addiction — any addiction. Any bump in the road of life, any psychic scrape or emotional bruise can reverse years of progress."

"I think I understand," I replied.

"Do you?" Dr. Nablaum said. "If you truly do, then you understand how Anna Worth suffered at the hands of that yellow journalist — that, that scandalmonger, Timothy Brennan!"

I was a little taken aback by Dr. Nablaum's passion. Maybe I should be considering *him* a suspect.

Not likely, Jack said. *He's steamed, all right, but I don't make him for the killer. Or Anna. I've been eavesdropping on them since they toddled in. What you see is what you get — a frail frail and a low-rent head doctor who's found his golden goose.*

"Sad," I thought.

Yeah, this broad's a bundle of nerve endings. You can't tell me she had the cool to poison Brennan and then remain calm when your local cops showed up asking questions. And that's not even counting the fact that her doctor is a solid alibi.

I considered Jack's logic. "Okay," I thought, "maybe *she* didn't do it. Maybe she *hired* someone. She has the money."

Then why show up in the store on the night of the murder? Why implicate herself?

Maybe she wanted to witness the death with her own eyes.

Then why return to the scene and risk raising red flags?

"I guess you have a point," I silently admitted.

Meanwhile, the doctor was going on about Anna's condition. "Every time Anna made progress, a new article dredging up her past and opening old wounds would appear. Months of progress would fall away as poor Anna would sink again."

"I see," I said.

"All Anna wanted to do was unburden herself. Tell Brennan how he harmed her, and how she forgives him."

"It's part of my twelve-step program," she said, gazing at Dr. Nablaum with something akin to awe.

I bit the inside of my cheek. The way she'd said "twelve-step program" so seriously and so reverently, I got the impression she'd never heard of it before she hooked up with Dr. Nablaum. I wondered in passing what he was charging her.

More than he's worth.

Dr. Nablaum gazed at the heiress with eyes full of compassion. "For Anna, there can be no closure now."

"That's right," said Anna. "Now I can

never say the things I need to say to Timothy Brennan."

Tell her to say it anyway, Jack said. *Take it from me, the dead can hear.*

I told Anna what Jack said (not mentioning, of course, that the advice actually came from a dead guy). Anna and her doctor considered my suggestion.

"Take all the time you need," I said, pointing to the community events space. There, the carved oak podium still stood — a good enough stand-in for Brennan, I figured, since I was fairly certain that Jack was the only spirit haunting the bookstore.

I returned to the counter, where Seymour and Sadie looked at me expectantly. Before I could say a word, Fiona Finch burst through the door and hurried up to the counter.

"The State Police have been at my inn for the past two hours," she declared.

"My God!" Sadie cried. "Whatever for?"

"A Criminal Investigation Unit showed up with a warrant. They searched the Frankens' guest room from top to bottom. Then two detectives arrested Deirdre Franken for the murder of her father!"

Chapter 18

To Quibble or Not to Quibble

I dislike arguments of any kind. They are always vulgar, and often convincing.

— Oscar Wilde

"Okay, folks, I think everyone's here who's gonna be. Let's get started."

In so many words, Bud Napp called to order the emergency meeting of the Quindicott Business Owners' Association — or, as Sadie and I liked to call it, the Quibble Over Anything gang.

It was Sunday night, the store was closed, and the group of us were seated on the circle of padded folding chairs I'd set up in the community events space.

"Can we dispense with the roll call tonight?" Fiona Finch asked.

"I'm sorry, Fiona," said Professor J. Brainert Parker, "but as this association's secretary, it's my duty to take accurate minutes."

"Then mark me down as present and let's get on with it," said Bud.

"Cranberry Street Hardware is represented," said Brainert, typing away on his laptop.

"And *me*," said Fiona Finch with an annoyed sigh.

"Finch's Inn," said Brainert. "That notorious den of iniquity that spawned today's raid by the *federales*."

"Not funny," Fiona huffed.

"Cooper Family Bakery," said Milner.

"Sorry about the Oreos, everyone," Linda blurted.

Milner turned to his wife. "I already explained we were out of baked goods."

"I know, Mil. But *Oreos?*"

"What's wrong with Oreos?" said Milner defensively. "Everyone likes Oreos."

"You could have at least bought Entenmann's," she told him. "Or even Pepperidge Farms."

"Everyone likes Oreos," repeated Milner. He turned to the group. "Don't you all like Oreos?"

Everyone generally stared a moment. Scattershot nods followed.

Brainert cleared his throat. "Let's stay on topic, shall we?"

Sadie rolled her eyes. "Didja type in Buy the Book?" she asked. "I mean, since you're *sitting* in it."

"Yes, of course," said Brainert testily. "And my own business concern has been logged as well."

Brainert was one of four investors who, about eleven months back, had bought the old two-screen Movie Town Theater at the end of Cranberry Street. The place had been closed for years, and its ripped seats, filthy floor, and cracked candy counter had long been in dire need of repair. No bank would lend them the money to refurbish, so the renovations were slow-going.

"Not present are Colleen's Beauty Shop, Sam's Seafood Shack, Franzetti's Pizza Place, Koh's Grocery, and —"

"I chatted with everyone else today," said Bud. "Consider me their proxy."

"Hey, there, I made it!" called a voice from the door.

"Oh, hey, Seymour, come on in," said Sadie.

"There's our big winner," teased Bud. "And I thought celebrities like you were too busy on weekends to bother with us little people."

"Wouldn't miss it, Bud! Besides, I'm out of ice cream."

On evenings and weekends, Seymour liked to drive an ice cream truck around Old Q. He'd purchased it with part of his big winnings on *Jeopardy!* the year before. Apparently it had always been his dream to become an ice cream man, or so he said. Go figure.

"I parked the empty truck outside," Seymour said. "Not for nothing, but I never ran out of cones and dishes before! And that horde at the bookstore this morning? What a crazy day!"

"Thanks again for your help earlier," I told him. "You really saved our hides."

"Oh, my, yes," said Aunt Sadie. "And you get the next *four* pulps for free."

"Let's get on with it, shall we?" said Bud.

" 'Bout time," said Fiona. "That all right with *you*, Brainert?"

"I don't appreciate your tone, Fiona."

"What tone?"

"You know what tone."

"I didn't use any tone."

"Enough!" cried Sadie. "Get to the emergency issue, please."

"Parking," said Bud.

(Actually, what Bud said was *"pahkin' "* — his pronunciations displaying the dropped *R*'s and drawn-out vowels typical of many Rhode Islanders. But, as I noted much earlier, I'm sticking with the conventional spellings!)

"Parking!" repeated Fiona. "That's what I'm talking about! Today I had cars jamming my parking lot that don't belong there. Rev. Waterman had to post guards to see that there was no illegal parking in the church lot. Why, even the Embry land was vandalized —"

"I think 'appropriated' is a better term," interjected Brainert.

"Right on," said Bud Napp.

"Really," sniffed Fiona. "Someone tore down the fence. No matter how you feel,

246

that's no way to solve the town's parking problem! We're here to find a solution, aren't we?"

Aunt Sadie rose. "Look," she said, "we don't expect an author to be murdered in our store every other weekend. Nor do we expect to make national headlines and the news networks. This whole incident is going to blow over in the next few days, and then Quindicott can happily fall back into the coma from which it will most likely never emerge."

"Not if you're cagey, Sadie," said Seymour. "There are ways to exploit this incident, draw it out, make it pay long-term. Like the arrest today — of Brennan's daughter. That means more headlines, which means the crowds will be back here again tomorrow, not to mention the television cameras. That's our chance to make the first move. . . ."

Everyone leaned forward with anticipation, waiting for Seymour to continue. In truth, Seymour had always had far-fetched ideas. But now, with the *Jeopardy!* win, people actually took him seriously.

"Let's look at the facts," he said. "Firstly, the real Jack Shepard vanished in Quindicott decades ago. Secondly, the author of Jack Shepard's fictional adventures drops dead in the very same town — probably on the very same *premises*. Now, that's a Stephen King story."

Brainert frowned. "Except King isn't

writing anymore."

"That's not my point," said Seymour.

"Then what is?" asked Brainert.

"Here's a story Sadie and Penelope could sell to Hollywood as *Buy the Book: The True Story.* That'll keep this town on the map for years to come. Heck, those Hollywood types might even come here to film it."

Silence followed. Sadie and I glanced nervously at each other in a sort of "Is he joking?" way.

Brainert cleared his throat. "While Seymour's idea is . . . interesting, I'm not sure what it has to do with parking."

"It has nothing to do with parking," Bud Napp said, rising. "But who cares? A murder involving a best-selling author is much more interesting than Quindicott's parking problem!"

Then Bud turned to Fiona Finch: "What *did* happen at your inn this afternoon?"

That's all the encouragement Fiona needed. She stood up, adjusted her bird pin, and launched into her story with gusto.

"The State Police arrived at around one o'clock, along with a Criminal Investigation Unit, and our local police chief Ciders. A Detective-Lieutenant Marsh showed me a warrant to search the premises. And another investigator — from the medical examiner's office — started grilling me about the Frankens. Where had they gone? When were they coming back? I told him they'd gone to lunch in Newport — because, of course, we don't have *one* decent restaurant in this town —"

"Stay on the subject," said Bud.

"Well, you know how I feel about it —"

"We know!" cried half the room. Fiona's decades-long reverie of opening up a gourmet restaurant at Finch's Inn was as ubiquitous a notion as Harriet McClure's self-portraits — and the wasted Embry lot.

"Just get on with it," said Brainert.

"Fine," snipped Fiona. "At that point, the search began. And within half an hour, I saw a woman from the Criminal Investigation Unit carrying a disposable syringe in a clear plastic bag to their police van."

Hearing that last line, I nearly choked on my Oreo.

Could the syringe found in Mrs. Franken's possession be a *second* syringe? I wondered. No, I decided. *That* would be too much of a coincidence. It *had* to be the same syringe. For some reason, Josh must have planted it in the Frankens' room.

Now you're thinking, said Jack in my head.

"A syringe?" said Brainert.

Fiona nodded. "I got a pretty good look at it, then I heard the detectives talking about dusting the syringe for fingerprints and testing the residue inside, so I knew what they'd found."

"Poison!" Seymour declared. Fiona nodded and smiled smugly. It was, after all, her theory voiced that very morning that Seymour was now endorsing.

"It's *got* to be poison," he continued. "Maybe it was arsenic — you know, like that church poisoning up there in Maine. The pot of coffee to die for."

Everyone began to chatter and toss out wild theories and rapid-fire questions. I kept my mouth shut, even though I wanted to scream the truth. For some reason, Josh Bernstein had set up poor Deirdre Brennan-Franken for murder.

But what was my proof?

A ghost saw Josh find the syringe in my store's bathroom, and he told me all about it. I wasn't about to fly that explanation past the State Police!

Crack wise all you want, sweetheart, purred Jack in my brain. *I'm your ace in the hole.*

Bud loudly clapped his hands. "Order!" he barked. "Fiona holds the floor."

"At that point, Mr. and Mrs. Franken returned from their luncheon," Fiona continued. "Detective-Lieutenant Marsh immediately placed the couple in the common room and asked them to wait there. Another State Policeman guarded the door. That presented a problem for me, so, *of course,* I had to go outside and creep around the house to the sun porch, where I could hear the conversation going on inside."

"Oh, *of course,*" Seymour blurted, shaking his head.

Too wrapped up in her tale to take Seymour's bait, Fiona simply tossed him a naked little glare and continued:

"Alone in the common room, the Frankens started arguing again. Mrs. Franken was very angry. I didn't hear every word, but I remember her specifically mentioning that she'd caught her husband having an affair. She threw it in his face. There was some quiet talk I couldn't hear, and then she started raising her voice about Anna. . . ."

Fiona looked at me meaningfully. "Deirdre didn't mention Anna *Worth,* the cereal heiress, after all. That theory of mine turned out to be a dead end."

No kidding, I thought, shuddering at my accosting of that poor, pathetic woman.

"No, this time Deirdre Franken mentioned *another* woman," said Fiona. "This woman's first name was Anna, and her last name was . . ."

Fiona paused for dramatic effect.

"Come on, Fiona," said Sadie. "Drop the other shoe, why don't ya?"

"Here it is," said Fiona. "As plain as day I heard Mrs. Franken speak the name of the other woman. I wrote the name down, though it sounds foreign and my spelling might be a little off."

Fiona drew a crumpled piece of paper from her pocket. "The name of the other woman was Anna *Filactic*."

"Filactic?" Bud Napp said. "Sounds Polish. I knew a Bob Matastic in the Marines. Nice guy. He was a Ukrainian, though."

"Filactic you said?" Seymour cried. "Anna *Filactic?*" He rubbed his forehead. "My God, Fiona, you've got to be kidding. *Anaphylactic* is not a woman. It's a physical condition. Mrs. Franken was talking about *anaphylactic shock!*"

Fiona stared blankly.

"Don't feel bad, sweetie," said Brainert. "Ms. Filactic may not be 'the other woman,' but it *is* very useful information."

"Yes," I said, "very useful. Timothy Brennan must have been allergic to something. Obviously, Deirdre believes anaphylactic shock triggered her father's fatal attack."

"What is anaphylactic shock?" asked Sadie.

"It's a type of allergic reaction," Seymour explained. "A sensitivity to some food or substance that causes the mucous membranes in the throat to swell and close up, thereby suffocating the victim. The most common cause is an allergy to nuts. Peanuts, especially."

"Oh, my, yes," said Sadie. "Peanut allergies in children are very dangerous. I remember reading a tragic story of a child dying after eating a cookie with just a few pieces of peanut in it."

"They say even kissing someone who just ate a peanut butter sandwich can send someone with the condition into spasms," said Seymour.

"Holy cow!" Milner cried, turning to his wife. "I served my five-nut tarts that night!"

Linda paled. "Honey," she said, "there is no way they can pin it on you. You didn't know!"

"But that's not a murder at all," Sadie said. "That's just a tragic accident."

These hicks are cracked. Brennan was clipped — planted by someone who knew him well enough to know how to make it look like an accident.

I spoke up. "Calm down, both of you. Mr. Brennan didn't eat a thing. He refused any and all food. Insisted on water only."

"And none too nicely," Brainert noted. "Pen's right. Brennan only drank bottled water. I watched him the whole time."

"Yes," I said. "The only bottle he drank from was the one I picked out and handed him. That doesn't make me look very good, does it?"

"But the bottle you gave to Brennan was sealed. The plastic unbroken," said Brainert.

I nodded. "I opened it myself."

"There are many ways to contaminate a sealed container," Seymour said. "I remember an old pulp story, published in the thirties, called *A Vintage Murder*. The narrator injects poison into a series of sealed wine bottles through the corks with a hypodermic needle."

"Enter the syringe," said Brainert.

"And remember that maniac in New York City a few years ago," said Fiona, "he was injecting sealed water bottles with ammonia, right there on the grocery store shelves. It's entirely possible —"

"Probable," said Brainert.

"— that such a method was used to contaminate the water."

"If Brennan *was* allergic to nuts, a tiny squirt of peanut oil in his water would do the trick," said Brainert.

"Nut oil!" I cried. "Yes, of course . . ."

The memory flooded back to me of waking up the night after Brennan's death, the night I'd seen Jack in the shadows.

You took a drink from the bottle, Jack reminded me. *The one you half finished after Brennan's death and put under the counter before the police came.*

And the drink I'd taken had reminded me of Milner's pastry. Now I knew why. But who set the bottles aside for Brennan?

"Linda, you're the one who told me about the bottles set aside for Brennan —"

"I didn't do a thing!"

"Calm down," I said. "I know you didn't. Someone told you they'd been set aside, right?"

"That's right, that's right," she said quickly.
The Quibblers leaned slightly forward.

"Well?" said Seymour. "Who told you? Spit it out."

"Deirdre."

The whole room erupted, as if Linda had just dropped the last piece into a jigsaw puzzle. But it wasn't the right piece — and I knew it. Deirdre wouldn't frame herself. Which meant someone else who was there that night had told Deirdre to tell Linda those bottles were set aside. Someone had *saved* that syringe for a reason: they'd meant to frame Deirdre all along.

"But what if Deirdre is innocent?" I blurted. All eyes now turned in my direction. And they all looked skeptical.

"Why in the world would you think that?" asked Seymour. "What's your theory?"

I told the Quibblers what had happened the night before. How both Shelby Cabot and Kenneth Franken turned up at Buy the Book long after closing time, and how I later followed them into the night. Of course, I left out all references to Jack's ghost, along with any mention of Josh Bernstein finding a syringe in the bookstore's women's room.

Privately, though, I made up my mind to track down Josh Bernstein and grill him like a raw T-bone. I told everyone what I'd heard — or thought I'd heard — when I'd eavesdropped on Shelby's and Kenneth's conversation under the streetlight. And I wrapped up my revelations with two conclusions:

"I think that the 'other woman' Deirdre was referring to was none other than Salient House representative Shelby Cabot," I said. "And, finally, I believe that it was Kenneth Franken, and not Timothy Brennan, who wrote *Shield of Justice*."

Chapter 19

Things That Get Bumped in the Night

I distrust a closed-mouth man. He generally picks the wrong time to talk and says the wrong things. Talking's something you can't do judiciously, unless you keep in practice.
— Casper Gutman (a.k.a. "The Fat Man") to Sam Spade in *The Maltese Falcon* by Dashiell Hammett, 1929

When I dropped the bomb about Brennan's alleged ghostwriter, I heard a few gasps — the loudest from longtime Brennan fan Milner Logan. Frankly, I didn't know what shocked the Quibblers more: that Kenneth Franken carried on an affair with a publicity manager from his publishing house; or that he'd penned Timothy Brennan's latest opus.

Either way, I expected such a charge to be greeted with a certain amount of incredulity. And that's why, before heading off to church with Aunt Sadie earlier today, I'd made a phone call to Brainert.

Reading Timothy Brennan's book the night

before, not to mention having that odd dream, had started me thinking about the book itself. And when it came to solving a *literary* mystery, Brainert was my go-to guy. I nodded my head in his direction and he rose to his feet.

"After Penelope tipped me off to her suspicions this morning, I went straight to the college library and checked out a copy of *this*."

He held up a hardcover book with yellowing pages. The white type on the black cover read *The Neglected*. A small frame of spot art below the title showed a man's silhouette, lost in a crowd, and the author's name: Kenneth Franken.

"Franken was more than Deirdre's wife and Timothy Brennan's son-in-law. He was also an author in his own right — a failed one. Franken's first novel was published in the early 1990s. The genre was 'dysfunctional family drama,' and it had been published by Salient House, back when they were an independently owned publisher and not part of a European media conglomerate. The cover copy states the author spent five years writing this novel, his literary debut."

Brainert passed the book around. When it got to me, I studied the back, which carried an author photo of the younger Kenneth Franken. At that time, he wore oversized horn-rimmed glasses — which he'd obviously traded for either contacts or laser surgery — and there were no silver temples yet in sight. He was just as model handsome, though, and the author was described as "an associate professor of English at New York University," and a promising young voice "who was single and living in Manhattan."

"How did you find this?" Linda asked in obvious admiration.

"I never forget a book," boasted Brainert. "If I never read it, I read *about* it. And if I didn't read about it, then I saw the book in the store."

I passed the volume to Seymour.

"Kenneth Franken's literary debut was a bust," Brainert continued. "His novel was greeted by tepid reviews and general indifference."

He reached into the shirt pocket of his pale blue button-down and drew out several three-by-five cards covered in tiny, cramped handwriting.

"*The New Yorker* said *The Neglected* was 'a flawed effort featuring a cast of uninteresting characters.' "

"Ouch!" cried Seymour.

"*Publishers Weekly* was kinder," Brainert continued, squinting at his own handwriting. "They said, 'Mr. Franken has a unique literary voice, and his novel contains some sharp observations, but too few to recommend this raw, freshman effort. . . .' "

Brainert shrugged. "So Kenneth Franken vanished from the literary scene as quickly as he appeared. But two years after the disappointing reception for *The Neglected*, we see the marriage of Kenneth Franken and Deirdre Brennan announced in *The New York Times*.

"And here's where it gets really interesting, because eighteen months after Kenneth Franken married Deirdre Brennan, the Jack Shield franchise — which had shown steady decline in sales and quality — was suddenly revived with the publication of three new Shield novels in quick succession. Each of these titles garnered rave reviews, as critics who'd grown bored with the series suddenly became enthusiastic fans again."

"Coincidence?" said Seymour.

"I thought so," Brainert replied. "And I didn't believe Penelope, either, when she called me this morning and suggested that Kenneth Franken might be the *real* author of *Shield of Justice*."

Brainert sighed. "My skepticism vanished this afternoon when I read *The Neglected*."

The book made its way around our circle and back to Brainert. He tapped the volume with his index finger.

"Now, remember that Franken's first novel had a tiny print run and was read only in literary circles — which was darn lucky, because it's obvious that Franken mined his

260

failed first novel for characterizations, descriptions, and situations for use in the last *three* Jack Shield novels."

I heard more gasps and cries of denial. Milner Logan was practically apoplectic.

"Calm down, Milner," said Brainert. "It wouldn't be the first time a popular writer had to turn to ghostwriters. Alexandre Dumas, author of *The Three Musketeers*, may not have written many of the novels attributed to him. And in the 1920s, struggling pulp wannabes like C. M. Eddy Jr. and Elizabeth Berkeley paid my ancestor H. P. Lovecraft to ghostwrite stories for them. Why, it's even said that in his heyday, Jack London bought story ideas from Sinclair Lewis!"

I smiled woodenly as I reminded myself that Brainert couldn't help it. The tone of a know-it-all college professor talking to dimwitted freshmen just came naturally to him, especially when he was worked up about the subject.

"Okay," Milner said. "So the chronology works. Where's your *proof?*"

"I would never make such a bold claim without evidence to back it up," Brainert said indignantly. "A close reading of *The Neglected* gave me all the proof I need."

Brainert shuffled through his notes. "For instance," he said. "Jason Carmichael, the calculating villain in *Shield of Night,* bears more

261

than a striking resemblance to Carmichael Fahl, the calculating father of the protagonist in *The Neglected*. Indeed, the two characters are described with nearly the same words.

"Carmichael Fahl had 'a shock of white hair and mud green eyes the color of a stagnant tarn' and Jason Carmichael's had 'a shock of silver hair and mud green eyes the color of a stagnant pool.' "

"What in hell's a 'tarn'?" asked Bud.

"A small lake or pool," said Seymour.

"Oh. Same thing then, eh?"

"Come on!" said Milner. "That's just coincidence. It has to be."

"How about this?" Brainert replied. "Tandy Miller, the free-spirited artist from *The Neglected*, was transformed into Candy Tyler, the free-spirited music producer for *Shield of Night*. The two characters share similar biographies, both lived in Hell's Kitchen flats described the same way, and they shared the same fates — both were beaten to death by their heroin-addicted boyfriends."

Milner was still shaking his head, but his conviction was on the wane.

"And then there's the suicidal bureaucrat Philip Breeland, who is transformed into the suicidal police commissioner Pete Land in *Shield of Honor*. Both characters even have wives named Maisy Donner!"

Brainert looked at Milner. "How common is a name like Maisy Donner?"

Brainert's string of comparisons continued, until it was clear to everyone — including Milner — that Timothy Brennan hadn't written those last three Shield novels, but hired his brand-new son-in-law to write them instead. And for his part, Kenneth Franken had splintered his old, failed literary work to provide the fuel.

It worked, too. Those novels sold like gangbusters — each a hard/soft best-seller. New titles probably would have continued to sell — as long as they were ghostwritten by Franken. If only Brennan hadn't announced that *Shield of Justice* was "his" final novel and that he was turning to nonfiction.

"Follow the money and you find the motive," said Seymour. "I still think it was Deirdre. She stood to inherit her father's estate."

"Maybe not," said Brainert. "There's Bunny, Timothy's third wife. I'm sure she'll contest any will that doesn't give her full control of the estate."

"That makes *her* a suspect, too," said Milner.

"Except she was nowhere near her husband or the bottled water," said Fiona. "Remember, a murderer needs access as well as motive. Bunny was back in New York."

"She could have hired someone," said Seymour. "A hit man from Planter's Peanuts, maybe."

"Not funny," said Sadie.

"We're forgetting something," said Fiona. "What about Kenneth Franken? With Brennan out of the way, Franken could resume his ghostwriting career."

"Ghostwrite for a dead author?" said Milner. "That's crazy!"

"Not so," Sadie replied. "V. C. Andrews has been dead for a decade, but *somebody* is writing new V. C. Andrews novels, because one is published every couple of years."

"Maybe they're written by Anna Filactic," quipped Seymour.

I was pretty sure Fiona was headed down the wrong path again. If Kenneth Franken used the syringe to tamper with the bottled water, I could see why he had to get rid of the syringe. But why would he hide it in the women's room? Jack had already pointed out to me that someone would easily notice a man going into the ladies' room in a crowded bookstore.

Then I remembered the way Kenneth Franken stormed off in search of his wife's makeup case yesterday afternoon — a makeup case Deirdre claimed was lost in the women's room! Could it be that Kenneth and Josh were working together, to kill Brennan and frame Deirdre?

I dismissed that idea immediately. If Kenneth hid the syringe in the women's room on the night of the murder, he could certainly have retrieved it when he and his wife returned the next day. And if he was the one who'd sent Josh Bernstein to retrieve it, then he could have told the young assistant where he'd hidden it and not forced Josh to search for it. And that's exactly what Josh had to do — he'd had to *search* to find it.

No. In my mind, Kenneth Franken was no more involved with the murder of his father-in-law than his wife was. Beyond that, I couldn't prove a thing because right now, Josh Bernstein was the only key to unlocking the mystery.

"Maybe the Staties have it right," insisted Seymour. "The money trail leads right to Deirdre."

"Or Kenneth Franken," Brainert countered. "With Brennan out of the way, *he* could have taken over the Shield series the same way Kingsley Amis took over the James Bond franchise after Ian Fleming passed away."

"Eeesh! I couldn't finish *Colonel Sun*," said Milner with a groan.

"Oh, yeah. As if every one of those Fleming novels was a masterpiece!" Seymour shot back.

"Boys! Let's not turn this into a reading group!" Sadie cried.

"Brainert did that already," said Bud, chuckling.

"Only to prove Penelope's point about Kenneth," Brainert shot back. "Look, Kenneth had a good motive for murder. Not only the franchise, but also the other woman. Didn't Penelope say he'd been carrying on with that woman from the publishing house? Shelby? Well then, Franken had a motive to frame his wife for the crime as well."

The room was silent for a moment as everyone considered Brainert's point. Fiona spoke first.

"So you're saying that Kenneth Franken might have killed his father-in-law, framed his wife for the murder, and is now poised to take over the literary estate and live happily ever after with his mistress? Why, that's so devious. So cruel. So monstrous . . ."

Then Fiona nodded with enthusiasm. "I like the way you think, Brainert."

Except for one thing, I thought to myself. A *woman* had to be involved in the murder in some way — because the syringe was hidden in the *women's* room on the night of the crime. "Right, Jack?" I asked silently.

Right as rain, doll.

"That lets Deirdre off the hook, of course," I quietly added, "because she wouldn't frame herself — and the syringe turning up in her room was too pat, anyway."

On the money again, babe, said Jack. *It's a big, fat frame job with Deirdre posing pretty in the picture. But she doesn't fit, and she didn't do it.*

At that point, the Quibblers' meeting degenerated into several private conversations and even a loud argument. Linda and Milner drifted over to me, Milner glancing at his watch.

"We're heading home," he said. "We've decided to open up tomorrow, after all, which means four in the morning is our rise-and-shine time."

"What happened to your day off?" Sadie asked. "You never open on a Monday."

"We do now," said Milner. "If tomorrow proves half as busy as today and yesterday, we'll make a killing."

I rose and unlocked the front door for them, my polite good-night smile fading. Why did Milner have to use that particular turn of phrase? I thought. But what happened next made the words almost prophetic.

Linda was apologizing — again — for Milner's Oreos when we all saw the scarlet lights flickering down Cranberry Street.

"I think there's been an accident," Milner declared.

That much was obvious. I glanced down the street to see one of Quindicott's three police cars. A long black limousine was parked at an angle. No, not a limo, I realized with a shiver. It was the van from Arthur J. Tillinghast Funeral Home on Crawford Street.

Just then I heard the siren. An ambulance from Rhode Island General — fourteen miles away — squealed to a halt near the police car.

I hurried outside. The night was chilly, the wind biting. Paramedics had jumped out of the ambulance and hurried to a spot where a small crowd had gathered. Whatever they were looking at was obscured by Seymour's ice cream truck.

I stepped off the curb, and Eddie Franzetti suddenly grabbed me.

"No, Pen, you don't want to see this."

Milner and Linda stepped past me and out into the street. Linda squealed and covered her eyes. Milner turned pale and led her back to the sidewalk. More people moved out of the shadows, and Eddie rushed to move them back.

Despite Eddie's warning, I moved onto the street. The paramedics were down on their knees over a crumpled form lying in a puddle. No, not a puddle. Blood. It was blood.

The side of Seymour's truck — which held placards touting Orange Push-ups, Chocolate-Covered Luv Bars, and frozen yogurt — was splattered with it. And the window Seymour sold ice cream out of was shattered. The side of the truck was dented from an object's impact — I shuddered to think of what that object was.

I heard voices. Snatches of conversation.

"He just flew in the air . . ."

"Don't know who he is . . ."

"One of them strangers . . ."

"It was Zeb Talbot. . . . I recognized his truck. . . . Zeb didn't even stop. Musta been soused again. . . ."

Officer Franzetti appeared at my side. "Go inside, Pen," he said. "There's nothing you want to see here."

"What happened?"

Eddie cocked his hat. "About half an hour ago, Zebulon Talbot reported his truck stolen from out front of the Quicki-Mart. He'd left the keys in the ignition and the motor running when he went in for a pack of smokes."

Eddie shook his head. "Teenagers, probably . . . it's happened before, though they don't usually pull this kind of stunt until the *end* of football season. Those high schoolers do stupid things to impress one another — and sooner or later someone always gets hurt."

Eddie's eyes met mine. Years ago, a stupid drag-racing stunt had cost Eddie a best friend and me a brother.

"Who is it?" I asked.

Eddie shrugged. "Nobody I know."

The radio in Eddie's police car crackled. So did the one on his shoulder. He flicked a button and listened to his headphones.

"They found Zeb's pickup in the Embry lot," Eddie told me. "Nobody's there, though. . . ." He made a sour face. "Chief

Ciders is on his way."

"What the hell happened to my truck!" Seymour cried, hands on his head. "I just had it repainted!"

Seymour raced out into the street. Eddie and I ran to intercept him. At that moment, the paramedics lifted the stretcher and moved toward their ambulance. They weren't in a hurry, and with the ghastly amount of blood on the side of Seymour's truck I could understand why.

"Wait!" I cried. "I have to know!"

Eddie nodded. He reached down and gingerly pulled the white sheet away from the victim's face.

Even in the flickering scarlet light and the blood-flecked cheek, I could make out the young man's features. The corpse on the stretcher was Josh Bernstein.

Chapter 20

The Girl in the Frame-Up

Pinning a frame on an innocent dupe is the cheapest, low-down dirtiest swindle of them all. Only a third-rate miscreant would do it, the kind of bum who's lookin' to earn two slugs through the girdle.
— Jack Shield in *Shield of Vengeance* by Timothy Brennan, 1958

It's a frame job. And pretty as a picture, too, with Deirdre trimmed to fit. But the charges are smoke and the case is a Tower of Pisa — it's shaky and not on the level.

The Quibblers' meeting was over, the mess from the "accident" outside mopped up. Spencer had arrived home from his cousin's Newport birthday bash via the McClures' chauffeur — mercifully *after* evidence of the tragedy was gone. He was so tired, I put him straight to bed. Sadie had retired, too. Now I was alone in the store, listening to interior dialogue courtesy of Jack Shepard's ghost. He would not stop badgering me on the subject of Deirdre Franken.

If you don't do something, an innocent kid is going to walk that last mile to the electric chair.

"The electric chair? You're living in the past. Almost nobody goes to the chair these days."

Maybe that's what's wrong with this Coney Island geek pen of a "modern" world you live in. Too many square johns take it on the chin and too few grifters get what's coming to them.

"Listen, Jack, I'm not comfortable with *anything* that's happening. I know Deirdre Franken is innocent. But what do you propose I do? Go to the State Police and tell them the ghost haunting my bookstore insists that Deirdre has been framed and the evidence planted? They'll either think I'm crazy or they'll think I'm guilty. And I'm not ready to make my son a de facto orphan, either way."

But you can do something.

"What?"

You can solve this yourself and find evidence they will believe.

"How, for heaven's sake?"

Use your head, for starters. Trace the murder weapon backward. Frankly, I can't think of a bigger flimflam than putting water in a bottle and charging money for it, but that's the grift on the table, so where did those bottles of H_2O come from, anyway? Who had access to them — before you opened up the joint to the general riff-raff, that is?

"The bottled water came from Koh's Grocery. Mr. Koh's son delivered two cases on the morning of the event. The cases were shrink-wrapped and well sealed. I had to use a knife to cut through the thick plastic. One of the last things I did to prepare for the event was pull the bottles out and arrange them on the goodies table."

All right. Suspect one: the grocer. We can eliminate him because I doubt your Chinese pal had a motive —

"Mr. Koh is *Korean.*"

I don't care if the guy's Samoan. Who had access after that?

"You're not going to like the answer," I replied. "Deirdre had access. Deirdre and her husband, Kenneth. They were moving the tables around because Brennan didn't like the setup for the cameras . . ."

I slapped the table. "Hey! What about the two cameramen?! Brennan was very rude, pushing them around. And they sold the footage after the murder angle broke. Those are good motives, aren't they?"

Rude works mainly for assault and battery beefs. People die because they're rude to a guy with a gun or a knife in a gin joint or crap game — not in a bookstore.

"But they benefited financially from the crime."

So let me get this straight. You figure one of those spool-junkies spiked Brennan's fancy tap

*with peanut oil, on the off chance that he's al-
lergic, that he'll get hinkey in front of the cameras,* do the danse macabre, *then croak deader
than vaudeville?*

"Okay, maybe that's not the best scenario,"
I told him with a sigh.

*Go back again to the night of the murder.
Take it step by step, from the moment the happy
author arrived.*

"Brennan didn't like the setup, so he bullied Deirdre and Kenneth to move the tables
around. Some of the water bottles tumbled
to the floor, and Deirdre picked a few up. So
did Kenneth."

What about our other suspect? Miss Priss?

"Shelby Cabot? I had to leave the events
room, so I didn't see what happened next,
but I doubt she lifted a finger. She's not the
type."

*And yet Miss High-and-Mighty showed up
yesterday, in the middle of the night. And a
rainy night, too, risking ruination of the hair
and makeup. She served you up some insult for
a midnight snack, and then she left.*

"That's right. Doesn't make much sense. I
mean, her affair with Kenneth Franken was
obvious from the conversation I'd overhead,
but I never did stop to figure out why she'd
come by in the first place —"

*Yeah, and he just happened to show up right
after she arrived, don't forget that.*

"What are you getting at?"

He followed her. Maybe because he was helping her tie up some loose ends.

"Oh, my God," I breathed. "Last night, when Shelby came here, she asked to use —"

The ladies' john — to "freshen up."

"I didn't get suspicious because she'd asked to use the one upstairs —"

Misdirection, babe. Made her appear innocent. Oldest trick in the book.

"Did you see what she did in there?"

No, I stuck with you. Franken was with you at the time, and I wanted to hear what he had to say.

"I remember Shelby was pale when she came back from 'freshening up.' She seemed nervous, too."

Because she didn't find what she was looking for. Josh Bernstein had already snatched it.

"I don't know, Jack, this is going to be awfully hard to prove —"

Suddenly a wave of raw emotion washed through me, and I reeled, grabbing the counter to steady myself against what felt like the wind being knocked out of me.

We can't let this frame-up artist get away with murder — twice. You and I know that hit-and-run tonight was no traffic accident. Brennan is dead. Brennan's daughter is innocent. And some peach-faced kid ended up as roadkill, maybe because he tumbled onto his boss's and her lover's plan and was ready to dish dirt to the cops.

I took a deep breath, not sure whether I

was more shaken up by Jack's reality check or the intimate rush of his intense emotions.

"Where does that leave us?" I asked.

If I were the hangman, I'd place the noose around Shelby Cabot's neck. Hers and Kenneth Franken's.

My heart sunk. It had been a disillusioning few days for me. First I discovered that a much-admired literary figure was, in reality, a cruel, bitter old tyrant who bullied everyone around him. Then I'd learned that the sour old man stole most of his ideas from a real-life detective, and that he hadn't even written some of the best work attributed to him. Now Jack was telling me that the very son-in-law who *had* written those novels — without thanks or credit — was probably a double murderer. From this set of facts alone, one might get the impression that a life in book publishing was as ruthless as a career in the Mafia.

"Okay," I said. "How do we prove to the State Police that Deirdre is innocent? And that Shelby and Kenneth are the real murderers?"

Jack Shepard's glee was a palpable thing, carbonating my veins like soda pop.

Call them up and invite them over for a chat.

"That's crazy! For starters, Fiona told me Kenneth went to Providence. That's where the State Police took Deirdre, and he's trying to secure a high-profile criminal lawyer before her arraignment tomorrow. Fiona said he'd be back after that to pick up the luggage."

The faithful husband routine, Jack replied. *Or maybe Kenneth was the one who stole farmer Zeb's truck and used it to run down Josh Bernstein. Either way, it works out better for us. You might not be able to handle Franken, but Shelby will be a pushover for a saucy tomato like you.*

"I'm no saucy tomato, Jack. And Shelby's no pushover. She's tough as nails and twice as hard. I butted heads with women like her during my eight years in publishing — and it was I who wore the bruises."

That was before you met me, doll, Jack said. *I can show you the ropes. And I've always found the toughest nuts are the easiest to crack. Poke a few holes in their skin and they deflate like balloons. You just have to muster the nerve to take a jab or two.*

"Okay. Even if I buy your mixed metaphor, how am I going to convince Shelby to come over here?"

Play the blackmail card. Tell her you have something she left, the very thing she was looking for the other night. Giver her the drift that you know the score, that you have the syringe. And this is key: make her think you're on her side.

"But I don't have the syringe. The police do —"

That's our ace in the hole. My bet is the po-

277

lice haven't enlightened Deirdre or Kenneth as to what they found yet — and no one else saw it except Bird Woman —

"Fiona Finch!"

— And that kind of information won't be made public until after the arraignment, if at all. So even if Shelby and Kenneth planted the evidence on Deirdre themselves, your mentioning a syringe will set Shelby's blood boiling because you ain't supposed to know. How could you? Unless you saw something.

In fact, as far as Shelby's concerned, you just might have the real *syringe, and the one Josh Bernstein found was a phony. Make her believe that, and you'll have her eating out of your hand.*

"Are you sure?"

Sure I'm sure! Even if she thinks you're bluffing, she'll know something's up — something that smells like blackmail. And if she thinks you have the real syringe, even better.

Shelby probably wiped the fingerprints off the syringe, but she'll still have doubts. Murderers always do, and doubts prey on guilty minds in the wee small hours. It gnaws at their edges, exposing the raw fear of being caught. You're in a good position to take advantage of that dame's night sweats. Dangle that syringe as bait and you'll get her over here. Then you can give her the third degree.

"I'm supposed to give her the third degree? I don't even know the etymology of the term."

278

Keep your panties on. I know the routine. I broke con artists, hit men, and nickel grifters as a private dick — and without breaking their knees, either. Well . . . most of the time. Anyway, I'll be right here inside your head, telling you what to say.

"I appreciate the offer, but I can't do it. I'm just not very good at being tough, Jack. I'm sure I'd just fold and mess it all up somehow."

There was a long, empty silence. A chill bit the air, and I shivered.

"Jack? . . . I'm sorry . . ." But there was no response. No voice. Not even a sense of him. Just a cold, empty room.

Suddenly, a hard, sharp series of knocks sounded on the glass of the store's front door. I jumped and turned. A dark blue uniform shifted from foot to foot on the sidewalk: Officer Eddie Franzetti.

I went to the door, unbolted it. "Eddie? What brings you back?"

He didn't speak right away. I didn't like the expression in his dark brown gaze.

"Oh, hey, I saved you a copy of *Shield of Justice,*" I said, trying to lighten the mood. I moved into the store and reached behind the counter. With a sharp box cutter, I opened the very last of the twenty boxes and held the book out to Eddie. But he didn't take it. Instead, he took off his hat and looked down at the floor.

"I knew you lied to me, Pen," he said in a whisper. "You said you didn't recognize that corpse. But I could see in your face that you did."

I nodded. There was no use denying it now.

"I figured you had your reasons, so I gave you a little time. But we still haven't I.D.'d him, so I had to come back." Eddie lifted his head and his eyes met mine. "Who was it, Pen? And why didn't you tell me his name?"

"His name was Josh Bernstein. He was a publicity assistant with Salient House. And his death was no accident," I replied.

"You should have told me, Pen. Lying just makes it worse. Chief Ciders is already fit to be tied that we haven't caught the driver yet."

That sounded like Ciders, all right. I remembered how angry he'd looked when he finally got to the scene of the hit-and-run. He'd come straight from Embry's lot, where Zeb's stolen truck had been recovered. He still had the lot's brick-red mud on his boots.

"I'm sorry, Eddie. I didn't want to tell you it was Josh because I needed some time to think. I just didn't want the police talking to Shelby Cabot. Not yet, anyway. Something's going on. Something I can't explain."

Eddie shook his head again. His face was so

grim I was really starting to worry. "Eddie? Is there something else on your mind?"

"I shouldn't say anything," he said. "I could get in a lot of trouble. But your brother Pete was one of my best friends. And your dad. He was the one who encouraged me, you know? Said I could become a cop like him, introduced me to the chief back when Ciders was still a patrolman."

"I know."

"They were good men, Pen. Both of them. God rest their souls."

"Eddie? Come on. You're scaring me. What's this all about?"

"I got wind that the State Police are going to be coming by tomorrow. Deirdre was arrested for murdering her father, but they think she had an accomplice. And since you were the one who gave Brennan the bottle, and they got it on film . . . I'm really sorry, Pen, but you're at the top of their list."

"You're kidding?" I rasped. My mouth had gone suddenly dry.

"Pen, just call a lawyer. Get some protection. I don't know how far they're going to go, but somebody really wants your hide. I'm so sorry to have to tell you this. Is there anything I can do?"

I barely heard Eddie's words. As my hand slowly set down the *Shield of Justice* book on the edge of the counter, I felt my body and mind go numb — except for one thought: My son. Spencer.

It's time, Penelope, said the voice in my head. *It's time you learned how to fight.*

"Okay," I said out loud. "You're on."

Chapter 21

Booked

She thought most men were weak and trusted her brains to slide her through anything.
— Ed Exley on Lynn Bracken, *L.A. Confidential* by James Ellroy, 1990

I put the call through to Shelby Cabot's room at Finch's Inn. After five rings, I heard Shelby fumble for the receiver and manage a tired "Hello?"

Double murder, it seems, can take a lot out of a gal.

"Ms. Cabot, this is Penelope Thornton-McClure." My voice actually sounded steady despite the fist that would not stop squeezing my stomach. "I'm sorry to bother you, but something urgent has come up."

"Mrs. . . . . McClure?" Shelby said through a yawn. I could hear the rustle of Fiona's silk sheets. "What time —"

"I found something in the store," I said. "I believe it belongs to you."

"I'm so sorry, but I really don't know what you're talking about," she replied, wide awake now. The woman's condescending tone had regained consciousness as well. "I'm certainly not aware of losing anything. Describe it," she snapped, "would you?"

Drop the bomb, Jack said in my head.

"It's an item you left here on the night Timothy Brennan died. I'm sure it was what you came here to look for last night. You seemed so upset, and I did want to help you, but Mr. Franken arrived and — well, I'd wanted to speak to you privately."

There was a long pause. Jack nudged me. *Go on, doll, you're doing fine.*

"Oh, I'm so sorry," I said with feigned bafflement. "I must be mistaken. I wanted to *help,* you understand? But this *medical* item probably belongs to someone else. I feel so silly . . . I'm so sorry to have bothered you."

"No, no, Mrs. McClure, I'm glad you called. As you know, I'm here to represent the interests of Salient House — and under the most unusual circumstances!"

Shelby was trying hard to sound cheerful. But even over a phone line, I could sense the strain. She let out a little laugh, but the edge of it seemed raw, like a section of scraped flesh with its nerve endings exposed.

"Timothy Brennan was one of our authors, a member of our publishing *family.* If this call involves the late Mr. Brennan or Salient House in any way, then I'll be glad to come over and settle this matter right away."

"Very good," I said. "Shall we say fifteen minutes?"

"I . . . I may need more time. And I'd like to first ask you —"

Hang up fast, barked Jack.

"Fifteen and not a minute less or I'll be *closed.*" I hung up before Shelby could make another peep.

Good job, babe. Now set the scene.

I did what Jack instructed, turning out all the store's interior illumination except for the security lights and fire exit signs.

Drunk tanks, interrogation rooms, and jail cells are grim for a reason, Jack told me. *Make this place dark as a dungeon. Pump some fright into her.*

Nature was cooperating. Outside, the night was moonless, and leftover clouds from last night's storm obstructed the usual burgeoning firmament. At this late hour on a Sunday, Cranberry Street was deserted, all the shop windows dark. I stood near the front door, peering through the glass. Behind me, the interior of Buy the Book seemed lost in a pall of shadows.

"Shelby wanted more time to dress," I whispered *very* softly, so close to the glass my breath was making fog. "Why did you make me tell her fifteen minutes or not at all? What's the point of rushing her?"

The time really doesn't matter. What does is that you set this parley on your turf, on your terms, and at your convenience. You woke her up in the middle of the night — she's disoriented, her judgment's bad. Right now she's stumbling down Cranberry Street, wondering why she's out in the middle of the night in the first place.

She's out there because you, Penelope, are pulling her strings like a puppetmaster. You've already taken control of the grilling session, and she hasn't even arrived yet.

I blinked. What Jack said about "control" was pretty funny, considering I felt completely *out of* control right now. But I had to admit, his interrogation techniques impressed me. They were nothing like the stuff I usually saw on television cop shows, where good-cop/bad-cop was often the extent of the strategy. That game wouldn't do me much good tonight. Sure, I could act the part of the marshmallow — but my hard-nosed counterpart was going to be out of sight if not completely missing in action.

"What next?" I silently asked.

Perps are all different, said Jack. *And different things get under their skins. Degradation worked on Nazi officers when we had to break them during the war. We tore off their medals and insignias, stripped them of their uniforms — even their skivvies. Butt-naked, even storm troopers lose their swagger.*

"Sorry to disappoint you, Jack, but I'm not ripping Shelby's clothes off when she comes through the door."

Too bad for me.

"Get on with it, Jack."

*Play off her prejudices. Judging from her treat-
ment of you, Shelby pretty much thinks you're a
doormat — a dopey dime-store hick. So act like
one. Play the dull sap and she'll get blabby,
thinking it won't matter 'cause you're just a
dump chump waiting for the bump.*

"Huh?"

Forget it.

Actually, Jack's words — the part before
dump, *chump,* and *bump,* anyway — *did* make
sense. Burying one's light under a bushel
was the biblical phrase. It was *the* tactic I
used during those difficult years in New
York City — at the office and in my marriage: unquestioning deference to authority
allowing conniving competitors and in-laws
to take their worst sniping slices out of my
flesh without saying a word back. That was
me, all right. I told myself it was the right
thing to do, the best way to evade the ugli-
ness of confrontation, and to avoid bruising
the fragile egos of my superiors, my husband, and my in-laws. I never set out to become a doormat in the process. But
obviously I had.

Keep things in balance, doll, Jack said,
breaking into my thoughts. *Doormats don't
raise a kid solo, and they don't take risks to
save a relative's failing business. You're no bum
taking a dive. You got the will, all right, and the*

heart, you just never had the means — or more like the meanness.

I wanted to reply, but Shelby Cabot was suddenly in front of me, just beyond the pane, her features pinched and pale under newly applied makeup, her short, raven hair scraped back into a tight ponytail. I opened the door and held it. She pushed past me fast, her eyes avoiding mine.

The door closed and I turned. Shelby stripped off her raincoat and draped it over a display. Under the Burberry, she wore dark tailored slacks and a cashmere sweater.

"Now Mrs. McClure," she said. "I'm here. Whatever *is* this about?"

Shelby Cabot's condescending tone made me want to shrink away under the counter, but I thought of my son and put on the mask.

"I'm so glad you came tonight, Shelby . . . *may* I call you Shelby? Good. And you can call me Pen. That's what my friends call me, and I do consider us friends."

Shelby's brow furrowed. Good. She was obviously hoping to intimidate me, aiming to take control through her superior demeanor. My sudden shift to cheerful, friendly friend seemed to throw her off balance.

Now get going with the dumb hick act, advised Jack. *Really start yammering. Talk her ear off, but don't give her a chance to peep until she's practically itching to shoot off her mouth, too.*

288

"I just didn't know what to do at first," I babbled. "I found this strange thing, and I didn't know what it meant or where it came from! Then I was watching the news with my aunt — you know my aunt, Sadie — and I saw the most disturbing thing . . . ."

My words came faster than the side-effects list on a commercial for prescription antidepressants. And Shelby Cabot's head was bobbing like a dashboard puppy's.

"I saw that Mrs. Franken had been arrested by the police for killing her father!" I continued. "You *did* hear that, didn't you? Well, that's such a strange thing to happen in a town like this, and what I found was strange, too, so I thought maybe because both things were so . . . so —"

"Strange."

"Yes — strange — that maybe these two things were somehow connected. And then there was that hit-and-run —"

Shelby's eyebrow went up. "Hit-and-run?"

"Right here in front of the store. But that couldn't really be connected with anything, now, could it?"

"I suppose not, Mrs. McClure. You said —"

"I found a strange thing? I most certainly did!"

"Where is it, then?" Shelby asked, her tone impatient.

"Where's what?" I asked blankly.

Pouring on the syrup a little thick, doll.

"Oh, you mean that thing!" I exclaimed. "Well, I guess I thought it best to leave it where I found it. . . ."

As my voice trailed off, I watched Shelby carefully.

You do scatterbrained swell, said Jack. *Just like Gracie Allen.*

I wasn't quite sure whether to take that as a compliment.

After a moment, Shelby squinted at me, as if she couldn't decide whether to be annoyed or disgusted. Then with the flourish of a woman completely confident in her superiority, she turned on her heel and swiftly walked back to the community events space, straight to the women's room.

Jackpot, baby. She's going for it.

I followed right behind. "I mean it was such a strange thing. So very strange!" Now I was Doris Day. "A strange, strange thing . . ."

Shelby charged right into the bathroom. I entered, too, squinting against the fluorescent glare. Without hesitating, she went right for the paper towel dispenser anchored to the wall. She popped open the cover and reached inside, behind the large roll. She felt around for a moment but came up empty.

Bingo, said Jack. *That's exactly where Josh Bernstein found the syringe.*

"Oh," I said, wringing my hands. "Silly me. You're looking for it there. I moved it the other day. Put it in a safe place."

"But I thought —"

Before Shelby could say another word, I spun on my heels and rushed out of the women's room, my nerves shaking as I raced through the large community events space and toward the register counter.

"Safe place!" I called. "Right over here!"

I exhaled with relief when I'd finally made it to the designated spot. Shelby took the bait. She was right on my heels.

"Where did you put the syringe, Penelope?" she said. Her voice was no longer arrogant. It was low and harsh. Ugly. Threatening.

I turned to face her, my hands no longer flapping, my tone no longer flighty. I forced my gaze to lock evenly with hers.

"Why Shelby, I never said it was a *syringe*."

Shelby blinked. Her confident mask faltered. I took a step toward her. She backed away.

"How many bottles did you contaminate with the nut extract?" I asked. "One or two? Or all of them?"

Shelby took another step back. Then she raised her chin and looked down her nose at me.

"Enough," she replied. "I almost laughed out loud when you personally handed him one of the tainted bottles." Then Shelby frowned, her eyes distant. "But I used a little too much peanut oil, I'm afraid. Salient House lost a very profitable author. But then, they were going to lose him anyway."

You nailed her, kid, now keep her yammering, get her to finger lover boy. Confess to being in on Josh's murder.

Shelby looked at me. "You probably won't believe this, but I didn't mean to kill Timothy Brennan. I only wanted to make him sick, too sick to make his asinine announcement —"

"About dropping the Shield series?"

"That franchise was just starting to pay off again. Even the backlist was moving. It would have been such a blow to my company —"

"To Kenneth, you mean, since it was Kenneth Franken who actually *wrote* those last three Jack Shield novels. The franchise was a success because of Kenneth's ghostwriting work. And that's who you really cared about, wasn't it?"

More of Shelby's composure melted.

Remember, said Jack. *Poke a few holes in her armor and she'll deflate like a balloon.*

"How did you find out about Kenneth's ghostwriting?" Shelby demanded.

"I can *read*, Shelby. And so can a lot of other people. I saw how he'd mined *The Neglected* to jump-start the Jack Shield series again. But it was only a matter of time before someone else — someone in the press — made the connection and figured out that the last three novels were ghostwritten, especially with Kenneth Franken accompanying Brennan on his author tour."

I watched Shelby's wincing reaction.

"Oh, I get it now. Bringing Franken along was *your* idea, wasn't it? So you'd have a stand-in waiting in the wings when Timothy Brennan collapsed. You were just waiting to drag Kenneth Franken in front of a microphone and reveal to the world that *he* really wrote those last three books, weren't you?"

"Kenneth is weak," said Shelby. "He refused to stand up to his father-in-law. Refused to promote himself and his writing. He's a literary genius, so he's far too sensitive when it comes to these things. It's a tough business. He doesn't understand how tough."

"I see. So you graciously stepped in, because Kenneth needed someone with brains to manage his career. Someone like you. And Josh Bernstein? How did he fit into all this? Why did he have to die?"

"Josh was always ambitious," Shelby replied. "But not smart. He figured out that Kenneth and I — well, you know what he figured out. That was bad enough, but he wouldn't stop there."

"He saw you tampering with the water bottles that night and then rush into the women's room," I guessed. "He knew you hid something in there."

"I tried to distract him, sent him off on that fool's errand for throat spray. But it didn't work."

"So Josh was never part of your plan."

"He had plans of his own. Blackmail. I told him I'd meet his demands if he planted the syringe in Deirdre's luggage. He did as he was told, but poor Josh met with an accident before I could return the favor. Not my fault."

My eyes drifted to the floor. Then I smiled. Shelby must be running out of clothes, because she was wearing the same shoes she'd had on earlier — I could see the brick-red mud from Embry's lot still on them.

"*You* were the one who stole the truck," I said as soon as the realization came. "You were the one who ran Josh down."

Shelby smiled, tight-lipped. In the dim light, with her hair raked back, her face resembled a skull. "You *think* you know a lot —"

"For a small-bookstore owner?"

"And as a small-bookstore owner, Mrs. McClure, you ought to know exactly what you're messing with when you mess with me. Salient House is the largest publisher of fiction in the English-speaking world. How long would your little independent bookstore survive without access to novels by Maxwell Cushing, Louise Harper Mars, Anne Wheat, and all the other big best-sellers we publish, along with their backlists? You don't have a syringe. You don't have anything. And if you make a nasty accusation you can't prove, I'll make sure Salient House sees you as a bad risk and cuts you off — completely!"

I shrugged. "Well, Ms. Cabot, I admit that losing George Young as a sales rep would be sad, but we'd simply place our order through Ingram. Or Baker and Taylor. As an independent store, Salient House can't very well tell those independent distributors who to sell to. And if they tried, let me see now — what would our hick-town lawyer call that? Restraint of trade, maybe?"

Shelby was fast losing her composure. Her empty threats weren't scaring the chick from the sticks. She glared at me, looking trapped.

Time to pull the trigger, toots. She still hasn't spilled her guts.

"So how could you do it, Shelby? Murder? *Double* murder? Is Kenneth Franken really worth it? You must really love him."

Shelby's brow furrowed; her lips slightly quivered.

"That's none of your business," cried Shelby. "Just tell me what you want. I'm sure we can come to some sort of arrangement."

Keep goring the bull, babe.

"Shelby, isn't the real question: Does Kenneth love you? I mean, if he really loved you, then why is he in Providence right this minute, trying to find a lawyer for his wife? And not with the woman who murdered for him?"

This is it. She's going to finger Franken as her accomplice.

"He'll come around," Shelby said through clenched teeth. "He loved me once. He'll love me again. Once he sees what I've done for him. Once I tell him. And I will, after his wife's good and convicted."

I did my best to maintain my composure, but I couldn't help at least blinking in surprise. "You mean it's over? Between you and Kenneth?"

"Not over. Just interrupted. He pretends to love his wife, but I know how he really feels — about her. About me." Shelby's eyes became glassy, creepy. "You're just like Kenneth," she rasped. "You eat the sausage but you don't have a clue what it takes to kill the pig. I used my networking contacts to introduce Kenneth to the right people, in New York and in Hollywood. He has an agent now. Because of me. He's in negotiations with Visionwerks to write a feature film because of me —"

"But the film deal is based on the Jack Shield novels, isn't it?" I pointed out. "And Timothy Brennan was the one who controlled all the rights? So his consent would be needed for any film deal to be made."

"Brennan was an egomaniac. And he'd become lazy. He didn't want to write the books anymore, but he wanted to take the credit and most of the money. And then he became angry — and jealous — that the books Kenneth wrote were so much better, so much more popular, than his own."

"So that's why Brennan was ending the series," I guessed. "He didn't want his son-in-law — the high-and-mighty ex-college professor — to show him up."

"He was a stupid old bastard!" said Shelby. "All Brennan had to do was keep his mouth shut and let the Hollywood deal go through. Everything would have been fine! Brennan would have made lots of money, and Kenneth would have started a new career on the West Coast — far from Brennan and that doggy-faced wife of his."

"Then you really *did* use the right amount of oil, didn't you, Shelby?" I said. "Enough to kill Brennan, because deep down you knew he'd never let Kenneth succeed."

"So what?" Shelby said. "I'm glad Timothy Brennan's dead. And you should be, too. Look what it's done for your store!"

Keep going, kid. Hang in there.

"I understand now," I said with feigned sympathy, trying not to throw up. "You did it for love . . . for Kenneth . . . and to save the Jack Shield franchise."

Shelby nodded slowly, clearly skeptical of my act, but hopeful, too — and desperate for an ally. "Do you see what I was up against, Mrs. McClure? Do you really see?"

"Yes, of course! A great literary talent like Kenneth Franken was being crushed by the selfish ego of a" — I nearly bit my tongue — "a foolish has-been. Somewhere along the way, you and Kenneth had fallen in love. You had an affair with him, but he went back to his wife, so you devised a plan to change the order of the universe, tilt the earth so he'd roll back into your lap, bringing the Shield franchise right along with him. How am I doing, Shelby? Am I right?"

Shelby's eyes narrowed suspiciously. "You seem to understand everything, which tells me that maybe you *do* have the syringe — the real syringe." She held out her hand. "Give it to me. Now."

"No, Shelby," I said. Slowly, my stupid grin flat-lined. Now it was Shelby's turn to yammer on like a crazy person.

"You can't prove anything!" she cried. "Even if you have the syringe. Why would I kill Brennan, anyway? What possible motive could I have? I'm not the one profiting from Brennan's death — you arc. You're the one who handed Brennan the tainted bottle, a moment that was caught on tape, by the way. Have you seen CNN lately? If I were the police, it's *you* I would arrest."

"But you're the one who knew how particular Brennan was about his appearances, so you didn't return my calls on purpose — to make sure there'd be chaos when you all arrived. It was you who set aside those tainted bottles and you who told Deirdre to inform the rest of us, so you wouldn't be implicated," I said when her tirade ended. "Of course, nobody will believe anything Deirdre says, given what she's charged with. But surely Kenneth suspects you. He might even go to the police himself."

"There's where you're dead wrong. I know Kenneth. He's a brilliant, attractive man, but he's far too idealistic. Too wrapped up in 'doing the right thing' to see that getting Brennan out of the way *is* the right thing. So I didn't involve him. Oh, he had his suspicions, even started questioning me that night he followed me to your store. But I denied having anything to do with Brennan's death, and he believed me. He knows nothing, Mrs. McClure. But even if he did have his suspicions, he would never tell anyone. Not after all I've done for him."

"All you've done," I said. "Oh, that's right. You made a few phone calls. And then, of course, you tried to wreck his marriage. Can't forget that one. And now you want to make him an unwilling beneficiary to a murdered father-in-law and a wife who's about to become a convicted killer. A wife he clearly still loves and has chosen to stick by."

I wasn't very good at condescension, but I was learning.

Shelby's face became a primitive mask of harsh lines and dark shadows. "I warn you, Mrs. McClure. In games like the one you want to play with me, I play to win. And I play rough. I noticed you have a little boy. Accidents happen to little boys all the time."

Steady, Penelope. Steady.

My fists were clenched so hard I felt my fingernails breaking the skin of my palms.

"And if you plan to tell anyone about our conversation," Shelby continued, "it's your word against mine."

"And *mine*," said a male voice. It echoed through the room so loudly Shelby let out a startled scream.

Officer Eddie Franzetti stepped out into the open. He'd been listening to our entire conversation from behind the life-size Timothy Brennan standee. Slowly Eddie lifted his hand to reveal his police radio.

"I alerted Chief Ciders to the frequency," he informed Shelby. "There's a recorder running at the other end of the line, and one right here in my hand, too. And if I know my dispatcher, there are at least seven more of us 'hicksville' policemen listening in on bands all over Quindicott. Just in case my own testimony isn't good enough."

For the past fifteen minutes, I'd been carefully tearing strips from Shelby's perfect little corporate girl mask. Now the remaining tatters had been ripped completely away.

Tonight, it was only Eddie and I and a few small-town cops who saw her for the monster she really was. But the whole world was going to see it soon. And that realization sent Shelby over the edge.

"You bitch!" she screamed, lunging for my throat. "You set me up!"

The force of her charge sent us both flying, right into Eddie, who tumbled backward, over a nearby chair. Penguin editions of Conan Doyle rained down on me as I heard Eddie's head crack into some shelves.

Shelby's fists began punching at my face and torso. I tried to hide my head in my hands, but it wasn't working.

Fight, dollface. Fight!

I drew up my knee, driving it into her belly. When she recoiled, I positioned my feet and kicked with all my strength.

Shelby soared away, crashing backward against the long counter. I didn't see it right away, but her fingers closed on a razor-sharp weapon — the box cutter I'd used to rip open the last carton of Brennan hardcovers.

As I struggled to my feet, I glanced toward Eddie, but he was out cold. Then I saw Shelby, waving the blade in front of her.

I don't know what in the world got into me, but I suddenly heard myself screaming,

"Another bitch who wants a piece of me! No freaking way!"

Then I launched myself. The ferocity of it must have momentarily stunned Shelby because she froze in place. My foot kicked out, connecting with the wrist holding the blade, and her arm flew back. But she reacted instantly, swinging the other arm down, and her balled-up hand connected with the side of my head, sending me into the counter.

As I felt a blow against my back, my hand touched the edge of something resting on the ledge. I blindly grabbed the object. Securing it in both hands, I whipped around, swinging it at my attacker's head with every blessed ounce of wrath I could muster. With a loud crack, it connected, and Shelby Cabot crumbled like the yellowed edges of a cheap paperback.

I stumbled, suddenly weak. Gasping, I leaned against the counter to steady myself. Down the aisle, I heard a groan. Officer Franzetti slowly struggled to his feet. He shook his head clear, then rubbed the back of it. No doubt there was a bump the size of a grapefruit forming — just like mine.

I watched him hobble over on what looked like a badly sprained ankle. We both looked down at the woman on the ground, then at the book I had clutched in my hand. When he read the title, Eddie burst out laughing.

It seems I'd smacked Shelby down with

one of the last copies of *Shield of Justice* — the book Shelby had been employed to publicize, and the very copy I had gotten out as my gift to Eddie.

"Good choice," said Eddie, "although don't you think *Crime and Punishment* would have been more appropriate?"

"And heavier," I agreed. "Of course, I didn't have much time to make my selection. Maybe next time."

Sirens wailed down Cranberry Street and revolving flashes streaked through the picture window, painting the back wall of the store in red and white light.

"I'm glad it's over," I said, massaging my aching back. "Thanks, Eddie."

"No problem," he said. "And hey, now that you're not in trouble anymore, I think I'll have time to read that Jack Shield book."

I handed it to him. Then I closed my eyes and silently thanked the original model.

Don't be modest, babe. You did the hard part all by yourself.

Rubbing his ankle, Eddie looked down at our knocked-cold murderer. "What the hell," he told me with a shrug as four Quindicott patrolmen burst through the front door, "at least we can honestly tell the Staties we did it by the book."

Epilogue

Usually female detectives are not favorites with men readers.
— "The Editor," *Crime Busters* magazine, December 1938

Four weeks later, October came to New England.

I don't fully understand how the cool kiss of fall sets fire to summer's green, but every year, without fail, the foliage around Quindicott burns in hues of gold, scarlet, and amber, just as it does all over our state. And, every year, thousands of tourists drive north from the cities to gaze at this momentous event — primarily because it transforms Rhode Island's woods just a little bit earlier than New York's, New Jersey's, and Pennsylvania's.

After everything I'd gone through with Calvin, Shelby, and Jack, I found that, like the leaves, I had changed, too. I was no longer green. On that brisk fall evening when I saw Kenneth and Deirdre Franken again, I was totally prepared to handle the store's scheduled event. I'd helped seat the packed crowd in the Buy the Book community events space. And I'd appointed Seymour Tarnish to guard the front door, where he could express his sincere regrets as he turned away latecomers.

"The sign says occupancy by more than two hundred and fifty people is against the law!" I heard Seymour shouting. "You got a problem with that, take it up with the fire chief!"

Deirdre Franken, hearing about the latecomers, hurried to the front door, where she passed the word to Seymour.

"Good news, folks!" Seymour yelled to the throng still gathering outside. "Mr. Franken has agreed to do a second signing, at nine-thirty. Come back in two hours, and we'll let you in on a first-come, first-served basis."

Kenneth Franken was just finishing up the national tour to promote *Shield of Justice*. Salient House had stood behind him, booking him on major television shows to talk about the infamous Bookstore Murder and the bombshell that he was the real ghostwriter behind the last three critically praised Jack Shield books.

Now Hollywood was not only bidding for the rights to a Jack Shield feature film, they also wanted rights to the separate story of Brennan's Bookstore Murder. It looked as though Seymour's "crackpot" idea to promote the store and the town might actually come true.

Of course, that meant more business for all the Cranberry Street Quibblers, too. I sighed. More business meant more profit, but our parking problems still weren't resolved. And judging from the present throng, the night was going to be another late one — and my feet hurt already.

Yeah, baby, said Jack. *But I like your gams in those pumps.*

I fought off a flush as I saw Spencer giving Sadie a big hug near the front door. He looked the copper-headed cutie in his dark suit — how could a kid be a heartbreaker in only third grade? By looking like my brother Pete, I thought. That's how.

Outside, I heard the short burst of a car horn, and I noticed the McClures' driver waving as he pulled the Mercedes away from the curb. Ashley had insisted that Spencer travel to Newport this evening to dine with his grandmother. Now that the summer season had ended, the McClure clan had moved back into their New York City residences. Theater season was on for the ladies who lunch, and their children had returned to their private schools, but this weekend they'd come back up with the tourists to see the fall foliage.

"Mom!" cried Spencer, rushing up to me for a hug. I knelt down and pulled him in. When he broke free, he said, "Aunt Ashley wanted me to call you and tell you that I wanted to stay the night, but I didn't."

"Oh, really? Why not?"

"I told her I had to get home for your big night, and if her driver didn't take me, I was calling you to send me a cab. Boy, that really steamed her up!"

I licked my thumb and smoothed away a smudge of something, probably a French sauce, from Spence's cheek. "But did you have fun?" I asked.

Spencer shrugged. "For a while . . . then Aunt Ashley started bugging me about living in New York City with her again, going back to my old school."

So my sister-in-law was still at it, I thought. Well, I shouldn't have been surprised. When "the princessa" and her mother wanted something, they were used to getting it.

"And what did you tell Aunt Ashley?"

"I told her nix to that! There's no way I'm going back to New York. I like my new teacher. And I'm having too much fun selling books."

Nix to that? I thought.

"I mean, come on," said Spence, "how would I finish reading all the rest of the books in this store if I wasn't living here? And besides . . ."

"Yes?"

"*You're* here. And I'd never leave you, Mom."

I smiled. Round One to the defending champ of motherhood. But I knew the boxing wasn't over. As Spencer got older, Ashley would find new, more intriguing temptations to lure my son out of my sphere.

Well, I was ready for her now. Since I'd met Jack, I was learning how to fight in whole new ways.

"Pen," Sadie called, "the *Shield of Justice* display is empty again."

"Fear not, Mother! Spenser for Hire is here!" Then my boy was off, racing toward the stockroom with all the vigor of summer green.

I rose, dusted off my nude stockings and black skirt, and wound my way through the crowd to get to the main store counter. I touched the shoulder of our new part-time employee — a freshman from St. Francis College, the school where Brainert taught.

"How's it going, Mina?" I asked.

"Great, Mrs. McClure!" She smiled through braces as she bagged a customer's purchase. "This is so cool! I didn't know working in a bookstore could be so . . . *exciting.*"

Freckles doesn't glam the half of it, said Jack.

I ran my hands through my copper curls. I'd used an iron to add some bounce, put contacts in for the night, and makeup, too — Linda even helped me find a shade of peach lip gloss to match my new silk blouse. Still, I was truly surprised to see men turn their heads as I walked by.

Don't be, sweetheart. Didn't I say you were whistle bait?

I walked back to the events room, where the crowd — sans Jack Shield costumes, thank you very much! — had become restless. My old friend Brainert waved me to the reserved empty chair next to him in the front row.

I wasn't sitting a minute when the room exploded with applause as they greeted Kenneth Franken, who entered with Deirdre by his side. The author and his wife walked together to the podium, then Deirdre took the reserved seat next to me in the front row. Fiona Finch, Bud Napp, and the Logans were seated right behind us.

George Young, the store's longtime Salient House sales representative, back from his cruise, introduced Kenneth Franken as the ghostwriter for the last three Jack Shield novels — and the author of record on *Shield of Fate*, a new Jack Shield novel due to hit stores next fall.

During a second round of cheers, Deirdre took my hand and squeezed. She and Kenneth hadn't stopped expressing their undying gratitude to me since Shelby Cabot was arrested. . . .

The day after I'd provoked Shelby into a

confession, the Frankens had insisted on taking me out to Newport for an extravagant dinner to celebrate Deirdre's release. We'd become fast friends ever since.

According to the Frankens, Shelby had been a college student of Kenneth's back in the days when he'd been a teacher. She'd always had a terrible crush on him, even made aggressive passes during that period. But Kenneth had rebuffed her.

Years later, they met again, through Shelby's work for Salient House and Kenneth's work for Timothy Brennan. In Kenneth's words, he felt demoralized by his father-in-law's treatment, so he'd been stupidly vulnerable to Shelby's advances. He slept with Shelby for about four weeks and then, as he put it at our dinner that night, "I came to my senses."

He said he realized that he loved his wife "deeply and utterly." As he put it, "I realized I was throwing away something lasting for something ephemeral."

But Shelby didn't see it that way.

She began to plead with him, stalk him, and even threaten him. Kenneth thought ignoring her was the best way to handle it. And by the time the six-week promotional tour came up for *Shield of Justice,* Kenneth honestly thought Shelby was over him. Instead, Shelby had hatched a plan she thought would get her everything she wanted — Kenneth, riches, prestige, professional acclaim.

"Things didn't exactly work out the way she planned," I noted that night at our Newport dinner.

"No," said Deirdre. "Now she's facing the murder charge I was facing."

"If there's anything I can ever do for you, Mrs. McClure," said Kenneth, "you let me know."

"Let *us* know," said Deirdre.

As the applause died, Deirdre released my hand, and I gave her a nod and a smile. She nodded back at me, then gazed up at her husband, who returned her gaze with what looked to me like abiding love.

I'd never seen anyone look at me that way, not even my late husband. And I couldn't help wondering about Shelby Cabot — the pain she must have felt in seeing the object of her adoration giving his love to someone else. It must have been like looking into the abyss, I thought.

Don't get existential on me, sweet cheeks. The abyss ain't so bad.

"Why, Jack," I whispered in my thoughts, "I didn't know you knew the meaning of the word 'existential.' "

Don't crack wise with me, doll, I can scare this room into next week.

"Rule number one: Don't haunt the customers."

Nix to your rules. And anyway, what's the scoop on Peanut Girl these days?

"The last I'd read of her, she'd hired a high-priced New York City criminal defense attorney. And according to *Gossip* magazine, the attorney is planning a lovesick twist on the infamous 'Twinkie defense' that got off Harvey Milk's killer —"

Back up, babe. What's a Twinkie? And who the hell's Harvey Milk?

"I'll tell you later. Just trust me that it's a stretch. The attorney wants to argue that Shelby couldn't help killing Brennan because she'd been driven temporarily insane by loss of love."

You buy that?

"Which part?"

The defense's strategy.

"I don't know. Sounds like a cheap rumor to me. Then again, I've certainly heard of stranger things under the sun. Namely you."

Gee, thanks.

"But the bottom line is, although juries in this country sometimes do deliberate irrationally — they seldom do it in the common-sense state of Rhode Island. So, frankly, I'm glad I'm not in her shoes."

Close call, that one. You almost were. But Shelby made a mistake — the kind of mistake only an uptown girl would make.

"What's that?"

Shelby thought she was in a town packed with

hicks and rubes. A bunch of bumpkins not so-phisticated enough to catch on to her slick act. She couldn't have been more wrong. Small-town folks are just like big-city slickers — some are dumb and some are smart. What's different about the big city and the tiny town ain't the size of the burg, it's the anonymity. No one knows anybody in Bigtown, so anything goes. In Sticksville, folks know the lay of the land and they know their neighbors. Not much gets past them.

"Well, it wasn't fun times for *this* hick, I can tell you. I got the impression you rather liked the excitement, though. Remind you of the old days, did it?"

There was no answer to that, and I sensed Jack receding. He did that from time to time, on a whim. What was I going to do about it, search the databases for a book on teaching your ghost manners?

Frankly, I'd take on all the ghosts in Rhode Island before I'd want to see Shelby Cabot's stone-cold eyes again. What really sent the shivers through me was the realization that Shelby never thought what she'd done was wrong. She'd gotten so used to rationalizing unethical behavior in the name of big-time business for the "biggest publishing company of fiction in the English-speaking world" that murder just became one more tool in her box of tactical tricks.

It was that realization more than anything

that made me feel differently about leaving those hard-nosed city offices behind. I used to feel bad — like I'd failed somehow. But now that I'd faced down the monster that environment had helped produce, I realized how lucky I was to escape. I mean, this woman didn't think twice about committing murder — while I drew the line at being rude to people. Sorry, but one of these things is just *not* like the other.

Hey, dollface.

"What, Jack?"

What the hell were you thinking, letting this riffraff in, anyway? Take a good look, would you? What a pack of lowlifes, skirt-chasers, and miscreants — reminds me of reform school.

"Rule number two: Don't insult the customers. They're what's keeping this life raft afloat. And you know very well that it wouldn't be half as much fun to haunt a vacant building. Or worse, a hardware store."

Sometimes I wonder why the hell I'm haunting anything at all.

That was a subject I had actually taken seriously over the past four weeks: finding the reason Jack was trapped here in the first place. I'd been reading books, hitting the Wendell University chat room, visiting the library. In the process, I'd made a few deductions.

"Your own murder is still unsolved," I silently told him. "That's my best guess. But whatever the reason, I'm glad you're here. You know that, Jack. Don't you?"

The moment passed with no response.

"Listen," I silently continued, "since I have one murder case under my belt, maybe I can take on another — yours. We worked so well together —"

You listen to me, doll. You were good, but you were lucky. Getting yourself out of trouble with detective work is one thing. Getting yourself into it for no good reason is something different.

"It's not no good reason. You could be trapped here because of it."

The men who murdered me weren't playing. And I won't have you getting anywhere near that case. As far as detective work goes, you're still a rank amateur. I can solve the mystery of my own demise solo.

"But in your current condition, don't you think there might be a distinct advantage to having a partner who's actually alive? One who can leave the building?"

Jack was quiet for so long I wondered if he finally *did* leave the building.

"Come on, Jack," I mentally pleaded, "don't give me the brush. I'm on the level here. With your brains and my —"

Legs, sweetheart. What you've got and I don't is legs.

"Okay, with your brains and my . . . gams, I think we can go far."

The silence felt long and empty as I waited for his reply.

All right, he said at last. *But only because you ain't hard to look at, and you're learning the lingo, too. But get wise to one thing, kid — you're working the charm school stuff. Leave the hard thinking to me.*

My smile was so wide even Brainert noticed.

"Pen, whatever are you grinning about?" he asked.

"Nothing really," I answered with a shrug. "The ghost of a thought . . ."

Jack never did like crowds, or blowhard scribblers, so with one last tantalizing breeze around Penelope's perfumed skin and copper curls, he rose up through the first-floor ceiling and into the second-floor air.

Near the window in Penelope's bedroom, the night wind brought him the scent of salt. He could almost see the gale whipping up waves, lashing boats and rocks. The sweet summer air was gone, replaced with the stink of dying leaves, the acrid smell of fires burning all over town.

Life, then death, thought Jack. Death, then life. And the wheel keeps turning.

Laughter and applause leaked up from downstairs. Jack was surprised to find he could actually take some pleasure from it — only because he knew Penelope was part of it, too. Yeah, thought Jack, maybe this cornball town wasn't so bad after all.

"I'll see you in your dreams, baby," whispered the ghost. Then he faded temporarily away, back into the old fieldstone wall that had become his tomb.

We hope you have enjoyed this Large Print book. Other Thorndike, Wheeler or Chivers Press Large Print books are available at your library or directly from the publishers.

For more information about current and upcoming titles, please call or write, without obligation, to:

Publisher
Thorndike Press
295 Kennedy Memorial Drive
Waterville, ME   04901
Tel. (800) 223-1244

Or visit our Web site at:
www.gale.com/thorndike
www.gale.com/wheeler

OR

Chivers Large Print
published by BBC Audiobooks Ltd
St James House, The Square
Lower Bristol Road
Bath BA2 3SB
England
Tel.   +44(0) 800 136919
email: bbcaudiobooks@bbc.co.uk
www.bbcaudiobooks.co.uk

All our Large Print titles are designed for easy reading, and all our books are made to last.

FL